The Legend of
the Landkeepers

The Legend of the Landkeepers

By

Rufus Johnson

Rufus Johnson

10-12-07

ISBN 1-58500-470-7

1stbooks – rev. 2/18/00

About the Book

Twelve thousand years ago people came to live in America.

They journeyed through a vast frozen area for many months. Finally, as they headed south they left the frozen tundra behind. As the people slowly populate the new land, they nearly starve to death on several occasions.

There is one young boy living among the people that is destined to be a great warrior and leader. But first he must make his own journey into manhood. He leaves the clan to find his destiny.

He is soon fighting for his life. As he learns to live off the land he gains a new respect for all the life around him. He even learns how to talk the animals. He befriends a huge Elephant that becomes his constant companion. Together they are the Kings of the Forest.

Contents

Chapter 1: Time to move.

"So, it has come to this," Bob Williams said to himself. He was riding with a posse, but he was not happy about it. The posse was here to evict the old Cherokee Indian named Charlie Landkeeper. But that was not Bob's purpose. He was with the posse to make sure no harm came to old Charlie Landkeeper. After all old Charlie had spent years working with the whites; showing them how to live on the land without destroying it.

They were outside waiting for him to come out now. Someone was calling out again.

"Charlie, Charlie Landkeeper, I know you're in there and I know you hear me. If you don't come on out we'll be forced to come in and get you."

Bob recognized the voice of the his father, who was the local sheriff. The year was 1838 and Charlie was a Indian living in Western North Carolina. For years the Indians had been forced to move west to a reservation. This was the final push that would one day become known as the "Trail of Tears."

Charlie was getting on in years. Bob was not sure he could even make such a journey. Charlie had told Bob that this day would come. Charlie had spent many hours teaching Bob his considerable knowledge of the wild earth. This knowledge had been handed down to Charlie by his father who had in turn learned it from his father; and so it had been for many generations.

Charlie had come to the sad conclusion years ago that his people just could not compete with the land hungry whites. So he had decided that he would take a white as his apprentice. However, he had not been able to find one who cared enough and was willing to apply all that Charlie could teach him to help save white men from their own harmful ways.

Charlie had even taken a white man's name. The name had been given to him by an oldtimer named Ben Wilson who was now long dead. The oldtimer had been smart enough to know that Charlie could teach the whites a lot about how to take care of the land. But he was so old and frail by the time he realized this he could not do much about it. Even though he had been able to convince at least some of the local whites to listen to Charlie and follow his examples. Those that had were much better off than the ones that thought nothing useful could be learned from an Indian.

Bob's thoughts were interrupted by Charlie calling out to the sheriff, "I'll be out in a few minutes, just let me gather some things together." He had already packed his things but he wanted to take one last look at his little cabin before leaving. Bob knew that Charlie's wife had died on this spot many years ago during childbirth. Since Charlie could not bring himself to leave her even after she died he built a small cabin and stayed even though white men were living in the area. He had adapted the white men's customs and abided by their laws, some of which were strange to Charlie's way of thinking. Yet he was still being forced to move away from his beloved mountain homeland.

Bob could picture the inside of Charlie's small cabin in his mind. There were only two small rooms. One room was the combined cooking, storage and living room. On the end wall there was a small potbellied stove for cooking and warmth.

Near the back wall directly across from the front entrance door was a simple wooden table and chairs. Charlie had fashioned these himself. There were a few items hanging on pegs in various locations around the room. The other room was even more sparsley furnished. There was only the single bed frame full of Straw, and a small table with a wash basin.

Charlie called out to the sheriff, "I'm coming out." He crossed the room, slowly opened the door and walked out with his bundle. The sheriff had a posse of ten men with him. All of them were wearing deputies badges and were armed with rifles.

"Charlie, I'm very sorry it has be this way. Believe me this is not my idea. Word has come all the way from Washington that the Indians are to be rounded up and sent to a reservation out west. As sheriff it falls to me to help round up the Indians." Bob believed his father. He had never known his father to be hostile toward any Indian. As sheriff he upheld the law whether you were a white man, red man or black man.

"Just let me say goodbye to my wife and I'll be ready to go," Charlie said. Charlie turned and walked to where his wife and unborn child were buried. He kneeled beside the grave and placed his hand on the ground. "This is not goodbye, my beloved, for I am nearing my journey's end and will be coming to join you soon," he whispered. Somehow, Charlie suddenly knew who his apprentice was going to be. It would be the sheriff's son, Bob Williams. Bob was one of the few whites who had spent time with Charlie and learned from him. All with the sheriff's approval. Slowly Charlie stood up and walked back to the posse. "I'm ready," he said.

The sheriff turned and looked at his son for a long Moment. "Are you sure he asked?"

Bob took off his badge and handed it to his father, then shook his father's hand. "Yes; it is time to make my own way in the world," he replied. Bob was a strong young man. He stood six feet tall, and had broad shoulders. He was even bigger than the sheriff who was a big man in his own right.

Yet Bob did not try to show off, he obeyed his father, even though he did not always agree with him.

The sheriff nodded and turned back to face Charlie.

"Charlie; I talked it over with my son, and we decided that he'll accompany you on your journey. Not as your captor but as your helper and also to do what he can for all the others going on this journey with you. As sheriff I have had to spend long periods away from home. I know you always did what you could to look after my son while I was gone. Bob is almost eighteen years old now and he wants to see the great West," the sheriff said.

Somehow, Charlie knew this before the sheriff spoke. He nodded his head. "It's not necessary for Bob to accompany me," he replied.

"But I want to go!" Bob quickly said.

Charlie looked at Bob, "so it will be," he said.

Charlie was an old man, but suddenly he looked years younger.

Finally he had someone that he could pass his knowledge on to. He was already well on the way as it was. Young Bob had spent many hours hunting and camping with Charlie already.

The Sheriff mounted up and called for his posse to move out. The posse moved off slowly. They were tired and really beginning to get bored with this whole thing of making people move off their land.

Chapter 2: Charlie has a story to tell.

Charlie looked up at the sky for a long time. Dark Clouds were gathering in the east, moving slowly toward them and the sun was soon covered. Finally, he said, "It's going to snow again." Upon hearing this, Bob just shook his head thinking, what kind of mess have I gotten myself into?

There was already four inches on the ground from the snow they had day before yesterday. It's only been five days since we set off from Charlie's cabin and already I feel ten years older.

Even though he had ridden a horse almost every day since learning to ride when he was six years old, he was not prepared for the punishment his body had taken these last few days. He looked at Charlie who seemed like a rock that never changed. How does Charlie do it? He does not seem to be affected at all by all this riding and the cold. In truth Charlie was feeling just as bad as Bob did. However he would not complain or let on in any way that he ached in every bone in his old body.

Suddenly, Charlie reined his horse to a stop and held up his hand for silence. They were just starting to descend down out of the mountains of Tennessee. The elevation here was well over four thousand feet. The driving wind had blown the snow into high drifts in every deep depression or crevice on the mountain side. About 100 yards away a herd of whitetail deer were trying to cross just such a drift. The snow was up to their shoulders forcing them to plow through at a snail's pace. Bob quickly realized that he could shoot almost all of the deer before they could get back to safety.

Here was meat for the taking, and since their supplies were already running low he intended to make the best of the situation. He could already taste the deer stew he would fix tonight. He pulled out his rifle and started shooting as fast as he could aim. He had shot two and was aiming for a third when he suddenly stopped shooting.

5

What was he doing, Charlie had taught him to respect all wildlife. They had just as much right to life as humans.

Like Charlie said, "To kill for food was natural, but to kill for pleasure or to kill more than you could use was wrong and wasteful."

Charlie nodded his head in approval and got off his horse. Bob understood his intentions immediately. They had taken what they needed from the deer. Now they would help the rest of the deer to escape from the deep snow drifts. He and Charlie spent the next several hours cutting a path through the snow drifts so the deer could move freely from one side of the cut to the other.

Afterwards, Charlie started cleaning the two deer that Bob had shot. With skillful hands he cleaned them and prepared them for travel." We need to find shelter for the night," Charlie said. They tied the packed meat behind their saddles and started on.

It was getting colder and already there were a few snow flakes coming down. If they didn't find shelter soon they would freeze. Just when Bob thought he could not go any farther Charlie suddenly turned up a small side canyon.

Charlie spoke up for Bob's benefit, "I know this place, my father showed it to me when I was a little boy. Before I took a wife I spent several summers here. There's a large crack in the mountain with overhanging boulders that will protect us from the weather."

They found it just in time. The wind was howling and the snow was swirling down so fast Bob could hardly see ten feet in front of him. Bob quickly unsaddled the horses and staked them in the widest part of the over hanging shelter.

They were not completely sheltered, but it would at least keep them out of the snow. Just as he finished Charlie came in with a huge armload of wood to make a fire.

Bob decided to rest a few minutes before trying to cook supper. He leaned against the back wall of rock and closed his eyes. The last thing he heard before going to sleep was the cracking sound of burning wood in the small campfire Charlie had built.

"Mother, that stew sure smells good, when will it be ready?" Bob opened his eyes and was startled at first.

Where am I? he thought. Then he saw the horses and the snow beyond and remembered. He was holed up in a large overhang with Charlie. He had been dreaming, but he still smelled stew. Looking around he saw that it was early morning; he had been so tired that he had slept the whole night through.

Charlie had a pot going over the camp fire and was working on the two deer hides. The hides would make two fine jackets. Bob wondered to himself for the thousandth time, does Charlie ever sleep or get tired.

Upon seeing Bob was awake, Charlie said, "The stew will be ready shortly. When I got up this morning I decided to let you sleep, you looked very tired. Go feed the horses, there's no grass here." Bob wearily got up and went to the horses and gave each a double handful of oats. At this rate they would be out of oats in a matter of days. He gave each horse a quick rubdown and looked them over to make sure they were in good shape. Regardless of how tired or hungry he was, he was learning what Charlie knew all along. If you wanted a good horse, treat your horse good.

Bob returned to the fire and filled two bowls with stew for him and Charlie. "Charlie, how long will this storm last?" he asked.

Charlie replied, "Only one more day or so. Even though It's late December, the worst of winter is yet to come. We'll use the time to get ourselves and the horses rested up before we move on. Later today we'll work on the two coats I'm making out of the deer hides."

Bob leaned back against the wall, thinking. Tomorrow or maybe the next day they could move on. He was worried about Charlie. After looking closely he could see that Charlie was indeed suffering from all the punishment that he had been through for the last week. Bob could see that Charlie's face was a bit drawn, and his breathing seemed to be a little erratic. By the time they had made coats out of the deer hides it was time for the evening meal. They each had another helping of deer stew. And then Charlie laid down by the time it was dark and went to sleep. Charlie had also started coughing a little. He might be coming down with a cold, and under these conditions that could be deadly. At least Charlie had been right about the snowstorm, it

7

appeared to be breaking up. Well there was nothing to do now but get some sleep. They would see how things were in the morning.

Bob awoke the next morning to the sound of the horses stamping and blowing. The morning was bright and clear. Even though it was below freezing it would warm up to above the freezing mark by noon. The storm had dumped an additional foot of snow on the mountains. He looked around and was surprised to see that Charlie had not gotten up yet. Well after all, Charlie is the old man here, he thought. It's time I started pulling my weight around here. He felt surprisingly refreshed this morning. Even though the last week had been long and rough he felt that he was getting stronger because of all the effort he had been putting forth.

He decided to let Charlie sleep while he tended to the horses and made breakfast. He gave each horse another dip of oats apiece and gave them a rubdown. Going back to the campfire he saw it had gone out during the night. This was the first morning he had not awakened to a campfire since joining Charlie on the trail. Charlie must really be tired.

Looking around Bob realized that they had used up all of the wood smoking the deer meat. He would have to go out and collect more. He walked out of the overhang and was almost blinded by the morning sun. He shaded his eyes and waited a few minutes for them to adjust to the sun's glare off of the snow. When he looked down the mountain he took in a sharp breath. The view was spectacular. As far as he could see, the world had taken on a surreal white color. He had seen snow many times back home in North Carolina, but he was still surprised at how beautiful it could be.

After looking at the scene for almost twenty minutes he walked on to look for wood. Even though there was well over a foot of snow there was plenty of firewood to be found. There were quite a few deadfalls around that he could break branches off of. After collecting all he could carry in the snow he headed back to camp. After depositing his load of wood he made another trip to make sure they had enough.

Returning with the second load he heard coughing coming

from the shelter. Charlie was just getting a fire going, but it was a slow process since they had only a few small pieces of dry wood left and the wood he had brought in had to dry before it would burn.

Charlie started coughing again and had to leave the small fire and lay back down. Bob was becoming alarmed.

Charlie did not look well and in this weather the cold might cause pneumonia to set in. In this place that could be the death of Charlie.

Bob slowly added more wood to the small fire, careful not to smother it with large pieces. Presently he had a fire big enough for breakfast. He sliced some steaks off the meat they had not smoked and put it in the frying pan. It sure would be nice to have some eggs to go with it, but they would have to do with steak and bread for now. Even though they still had plenty of flour they were quickly running out of other food rations. If they had not come across the deer herd they might have starved before they got off the mountain. He realized Charlie was right again. You should leave something for next time, for there will always be a next time. He was beginning to realize that Charlie had been teaching him some very important lessons over the years. He had always thought Charlie was just making conversation to keep him interested. Now he realized the hunting trips he and Charlie had taken were more than just hunting trips to keep him busy while his father was away on one of his many trips as sheriff.

He removed the steaks from the pan and fixed a plate for Charlie and himself. Walking over to Charlie he could see that Charlie was asleep. He decided to let him sleep for a while, even though he didn't seem to be resting very well.

If they stayed here too long they would be snowed in for the winter. Even with the deer meat they would have to kill the horses for food to survive the winter. They had to be moving, yet if they tried to move before Charlie got well it would surely kill him.

Presently Charlie sat up and called Bob over. "Bob, my journey will end here. I am to weak to travel, and besides I wish to die in the mountains. I was born near here and I will die here. My body will return to the earth to nourish the next generation of life. It has always been so." Bob did not argue for he felt that Charlie knew what he was talking about.

"I have a story to tell you Bob. You must listen well and teach your people, for this is the story of life itself. Charlie Landkeeper is not my real name. It's the name given to me by a white man named Ben Wilson. My Indian name translates to Keeper Of The Land. That was also my father's name and his father before him. It has been so for many, many generations. It is a story of suffering and a story of sacrifices. It is a story of love and of learning. A story of happiness and sadness. Many, many generations ago our ancestors lived in a far off land. Things were much simpler back then than they are now. The people did not have the free time on their hands that people do today. The gathering of food and clothing was a fulltime job. People were known for what they could do and for what they did do.

They were even named for the way they acted or looked. For example, if a person could run very fast his name might be Runs Like The Wind. If a person knew what plants were good for medicine and which plants were good for eating and where shelter and water might be found he might be called The Wise One. When a person was given a name as a child, he might be given a new name when he was recognized as having a particular skill or if he acted a certain way. His name might even change several times in his life if something significant happened to cause his status in the tribe to change. Usually, the more times your name changed the higher status you held in the tribe. Most people went through life without changing names.

"They also gave the animals descriptive names. For instance, they called a rabbit The Long Eared One. But at the same time they had a word for rabbit. So if a person was named after a rabbit he might be called Runs Like A Rabbit. Yet when referring to the rabbit most people would call it The Long Eared One.

"The people had lived in this far off land for many, many generations. People were beginning to starve because they had killed off most of the wildlife. Then one day the land starting rising out of the sea. There was a great gathering of the people.

It was decided that some of the people would have to leave. They would go to the land that rose out of the sea.

"This way there would be enough food left for the people that stayed behind. No one was sure that they would find food in this new land, or if there would be bad spirits that would take the people in the night. However, if someone did not go they were all facing certain starvation. The talks went on for days. Finally it was decided that some of the people must leave or they would all starve. So the most adventurous and bravest men gathered their families and their meager belongings and set off into the new land."

Bob was transfixed by the story. It seemed as if he had gone back in time and was listening to the characters themselves instead of Charlie.

Chapter 3: The New Land

"I have no milk left," Deer Eyes screeched. "What are we going to do? I must have milk for the baby. You have to find food for us; my baby has to have milk." Fights With The Bear listened to his wife and nodded his head. He knew the situation was very serious.

He had to take action soon or their baby would die. Just then he heard one of the other women start wailing. It must be Short Woman. She had not had milk for two days now. He walked back into the cave where Short Woman was lying on the ground and holding a small bundle in her hands. Her husband, Square Jaw, was kneeling next to her with one hand on his wife's back. His eyes were closed and tears were streaming down his face. Their daughter, Deer Pawn, sat close by crying silently to herself.

Fights With The Bear knew what had happened. Their baby was no more of this world. He was only ten moons old.

With no milk in the last two days and very little before that, it had starved to death. The whole tribe was on the brink of starvation. As other members of their small tribe walked up they began making a circle around the grieving couple. Fights With The Bear spoke quietly, "Oh great spirit, please take this small one into your arms and protect her for all time to come."

Each member of the tribe then walked up, touched the Child, and walked away. After everyone was gone the immediate family members would carry the dead child to the farthest reaches of the cave and stay there for twenty four hours.

After this, the child's name would never be mentioned again. When referring her in the future they would always say Short Woman's son or Deer Pawn's brother.

Fights With The Bear made up his mind. The tribe would move again. There was no longer any food here to eat. It was early spring and the coldest weather was over. Fights With The Bear knew it was time to break camp and move on. He went to see The Wise One and ask if he felt the same way. The Wise One agreed that they would call a tribal council and discuss moving on or staying here for another season. After all, the growing season was already starting and in a few weeks there would be berries and other plants to eat. Though every year there seemed to be less and less food close by.

The next morning the tribal council was called together and discussions started on weather to break camp and move on, or try and live here for one more year.

The Wise One was the first to speak. "We are gathered here today to make a very important decision. Fights with The Bear has come to me and asked if we should be moving on to find the herds of the Long Nosed Ones. I will turn the floor over to him and let him speak. Each of you in turn, will then be asked your opinion."

Fights With The Bear waited a minute before speaking, for he knew the journey ahead would be long and difficult. Some of them may even die on the journey.

"My brothers, we have to put our heads together and come up with a plan for the future. Our food stores are almost gone and we have not seen any of The Longnosed Ones for many moons now. There have been no sightings of The Bearded Ones nor have we seen any of the great Sharp Toothed cats.

Why, we haven't even seen any of the great flying birds that try to rob our meat when we make a kill. I feel that it is time to move on again. On our last hunt we walked almost three days south before we found any animals to hunt for meat. This was near the great hills. I say that we move into the great hills, for I think there will be animals of every kind here. There will be food for the taking just like it was here when we arrived six summers ago. I know that it will be a long journey, but what choice do we have?"

"Well, everyone does not agree with you." Fights With The Bear turned to see who was speaking. He was sure he already knew who it was without looking. He recognized the voice of The Lazy One. The Lazy One was sprawled out on the ground as usual. He was very big, but it was mostly fat. His clothes were worn very badly, and he smelled worse than anyone else in the tribe. "Why should we move? It is already spring time, soon there will be food for the taking. We have a very good cave for shelter and there is abundant water close by. I say we stay put, why should we pack and move just because you are tired of this area?"

Fights With The Bear replied, "I agree that we have a good cave for shelter and we have a good source of water close by. But what about meat, and what about hides for making clothes? There are no animals left in this area. We must have meat to survive."

Suddenly, Square Jaw jumped to his feet. "I have lost one child already, I will not stand around and watch my only remaining daughter starve to death. I agree with Fights With The Bear. If The Lazy One wants to stay here, I say let him stay here by himself. I intend to move on to better hunting grounds with Fights With The Bear." Square Jaw sat back down almost as fast as he had stood. Everyone started talking at once but the general consensus was that Fights With The Bear and Square Jaw were right; it was time to move on. Each person was called on to give his opinion. All but The Lazy One's two brothers agreed with Fights With The Bear.

Finally The Wise One held up his hand for silence. He spoke quietly, "The majority has decided, we will move on. And now brothers, we must prepare, for the way will be long and hard. Upon the dawn of the day after tomorrow we will go south to the great hills."

Chapter 4: The Great Hills

"My feet are aching," Deer pawn said. "I feel like I've been walking my entire life." She was walking beside Talks With The Animals. She wondered how he kept on going without ever complaining. Talks With The Animals had been given a very important job for someone so young. He was only fourteen years old but in many ways he acted much older and wiser.

Sometimes however, the kid in him still showed. But there was no room for that on this journey, for he was one of the chosen two that would carry a fire. While they were on the move two people always carried hot coals in a basket of damp leaves. These were used to start a new fire when they decided to stop and camp. They also carried a few small dry twigs and grass to ensure that they could start a new fire even when it had been raining.

Even though Talks With The Animals's ancestors in the far away land had known how to start a fire by striking two special kinds of rocks together, his clan did not have any of the rocks. Talks With The Animals did not know this for it had been forgotten somehow after leaving the far-away land. He knew there were still several legends that told about the far-away land from which their ancestors had migrated. His favorite one told about how his grandfather's grandfather had gathered his clan together and started off into the land that rose from the great water.

"Did you hear me, Talks With The Animals?" Deer Pawn interrupted his thoughts with her question. "I said that my feet ache. It seems likes we have been walking forever."

"Yes I heard you, "Talks With The Animals answered her.

"You must be strong, we have to keep going. We're in the great hills now, we'll find a place to live soon. Already we're seeing more and more signs of wildlife."

"I know we must go on but I'm so hungry and tired. We have not had a good meal for days now. It seems to be getting colder in the hills, yet it is the time of year that it should be getting warmer." They had even seen snow on top of the highest great hills. Talks With The Animals had also noticed that it seemed to be colder the higher they went into the great hills.

"Maybe it is just the great hills that make it colder." Talks with The Animals said. "It seems that when we get to the top it is colder, yet when we go back down the hill it is warmer. My father says that it is much warmer here than it is at the big waters where the clan lived before. Every time we move to a new area it seams to be warmer. My father thinks that every time we move south it is warmer, but I don't know this since I was still a little one the last time we moved and do not remember."

Fights With The Bear overheard what his son Talks With The Animals was telling Deer Pawn. He was very proud of his son. He was sure that one day his son would be a great leader of the people. He was also sure that Deer Pawn would be his son's life-long mate. His son was already considered more valuable to the clan's success than some of the grownups.

Fights With The Bear's thoughts were suddenly interrupted by a loud noise. It was the distress call of The Longnosed Ones.

A few minutes later Square Jaw came jogging back down the trail. He had been scouting ahead to find the best path to follow. The great hills were getting so big that they could no longer just climb over them, they were having to go around them. He and Square Jaw had been taking turns scouting ahead.

Square Jaw called for everyone to stop. He was very excited and could hardly wait for everyone to gather around.

"There is a Longnosed One just a short ways ahead. She seems to have fallen and broken her leg somehow. She must have been separated from the herd. She is alone except for a baby Long nosed One that is standing close by. This is meat for the taking. Everyone grab your spears and come with me."

Fights With The Bear gave a war whoop and took off after Square Jaw, closely followed by other members of the tribe.

He was not going to let this opportunity get away. The whole clan was on the verge of starvation, and one Longnosed One could feed them for many days.

Square Jaw suddenly gave the signal for silence. He

motioned for Fights With The Bear to join him. Fights With The Bear moved silently up to Square Jaw's side. Square Jaw pointed down the trail to where The Longnosed One was.

Fights With The Bear spotted her and saw immediately what the problem was. One of The Longnosed One's great hind legs was pushed out at an odd angle. She was trying to stand but the leg just would not take her weight. She sounded the distress call again and set down. Fights With The Bear knew this was still a formidable foe regardless of the broken leg. She would stand taller than the tallest man in the clan. If her mate were around he would stand twice as high as a full grown man! The males also had very long tusks, and then there was that strange long nose that reached all the way to the ground. The Longnosed Ones used this as and arm. They would pull grass with it, and reach high into the trees to pull leaves to eat. They even used their long nose to draw up great amounts of water and squirt it across their bodies as if taking a bath. If they got to close during battle that same long nose would wrap around a warrior and crush the life out of him. Any life that might be left in a warrior would be gone after The Longnosed one tossed the unfortunate warrior through the air. Fights With The Bear hoped none of the great male Longnosed Ones were around.

"What are you waiting for, why haven't you killed the Longnosed One yet?" The Lazy One demanded. He had just arrived at the scene to see Fights With The Bear and the other warriors hiding in the bushes watching the Longnosed One.

"Must I go kill this Longnosed One all alone? Are you afraid of one defenseless animal?" In truth it was The Lazy One that was afraid. He had purposely hung back when everyone had taken off after The Longnosed One. If anyone asked why, he could always say that he was going slow to make sure that the women and children would not get lost.

But it was The Wise One who answered, "Get down out of sight and shut up. We must make sure that the rest of the Longnosed One's herd is not close by. If they are within hearing distance they will surely come and answer her stress call. If we get caught out in the open when the herd returns some of us would surely be killed."

19

Even though The Wise One was the oldest member of the clan he had still beaten The Lazy One to where The Longnosed One lay in anguish.

Fights With The Bear looked at The Lazy One with a hard stare but he did not say anything. Fights With The Bear came to sit beside The Wise One, "I don't think that her herd is in the area but I think we should wait a little while longer.

"The Wise One just nodded his head and remained silent. The women and children were sitting quietly close by.

Talks With The Animals came up to his father and said, "the herd is far away. They have been separated for two days now and the herd has no idea where this Longnosed One is."

Fights With The Bear wondered how his son knew these things. He did not understand it; but believed his son told the truth. His son seemed to know what the animals were thinking and doing even without seeing them.

It was Talks With The Animals that had known one of The Great Toothed cats lay hiding in a large tree limb waiting to pounce on one of the clan members. It was his shout that had given the warriors time to react before the cat had even came down from the tree. They were ready for the great cat and were able to chase it away with no harm done to any members of the tribe.

Fights With The Bear went back to the other warriors, "We will attack now. Square Jaw, take three warriors and try to slip around to the side of the Longnosed One." When you are in position, show yourselves and make a lot of noise to get The Long Nosed One's attention. While she is facing you we will attack from behind. But be ready to make the kill. When we attack from behind she will turn her head to get at us. When this happens you must quickly attack her underside where she is vulnerable. You must thrust your spears into the heart and get out of the way. For even when mortally wounded she will still be dangerous until she actually drops."

Square Jaw picked three warriors and headed off. Fights With The Bear moved the other warriors into position and whispered, "We must be alert. When Square Jaw and his men show themselves we must attack at once or they will be in great danger."

A few moments later Square Jaw and his warriors emerged from the woods with loud war whoops and a lot of thrashing.

"Attack now, but be quiet, we want to sneak up on her." With that, Fights With The Bear ran quickly in for the attack.

He plunged his spear with all his might into the Longnosed One's backside followed quickly by spears from other warriors. The Long Nosed One had very tough skin and some of the spears fell off. But they did succeed in getting her attention. Square Jaw and the others warriors quickly ran in and plunged their spears into her underside. The last warrior tripped just after plunging his spear and The Longnosed One made one last desperate lunge and grabbed him with her long nose. She picked him up and threw him high in the air, then she collapsed in a heap. The young warrior landed with a sickening thud and was no longer of this world.

The young warrior had not taken a mate yet, so his parents would take his body and prepare it for burial. Fights With The Bear touched the warriors young body and said, "You were a brave warrior on this world. I am sure the great spirit will open his arms and allow you to hunt with him in his world." Slowly all the members touched the young warrior to pay their respects. Then his parents took him to be covered with rocks as was there custom when there was no cave nearby to place the body in.

The women and children came up and after thanking the great beast for supplying them with meat began to butcher The Longnosed One. Suddenly The Lazy One was shoved very hard from behind. He went sprawling along trying to get his balance. He stumbled and fell headlong into a great heap of The Longnosed One's dung. Everyone started laughing at The Lazy One, which made him furious. He stood up and angrily yelled, "Who did that?" Then he saw for himself; it was the baby Longnosed One.

Everyone had forgotten about it during the excitement of the hunt. The Lazy One's spear lay close by, for he had waited so long to attack that The Longnosed One had collapsed before his spear was needed. He grabbed his spear and said, "I will finish you off now. There will be some tender meats cut from you and I will have my fill." As he advanced upon the baby Longnosed One, Talks With The Animals quickly placed himself in front of it.

"No, I will not let you harm it. It is only a few years old and all alone in the world. Yet it still has more courage than you will ever have."

"Why you little runt I'll show you who is brave and who is not. I will blister your backside for this," The lazy One yelled. He charged at Talks With The Animals, but just then Fights With The Bear stepped up next to his son.

"Since you are so brave maybe you would like to challenge me," he spoke quietly. The Lazy One just stared at them with hatred and then turned and walked away.

" That was a brave and foolish thing that you did Talks With The Animals," Fights With The Bear said. "However, we are now stuck with a baby Longnosed One. What will we do with it?"

"We can keep it father. I will take care of it until it is big enough to fend for itself."

"And how do you propose to give it milk. Why it must take several of our water pouches full of milk everyday to keep it going." Fights With The Bear responded.

Talks With The Animals knew he had to figure a way to save the baby Long Nosed One. "But Father, his mother was already weaning him off milk. If we make sure he gets plenty of water and food he will live."

"And if he lives what will we do with him? It is a struggle just to feed ourselves, much less a large dangerous animal like that."

"He is not dangerous, he will obey my command," Talks With The Animals responded. "And he will be very useful.

Think of all the meat and hides and bone tools we will get from The Longnosed One. Why it is more than the whole clan can carry and there is no shelter here. We can use the baby Longnosed One to help carry supplies until we find shelter."

Fights With The Bear had to concede, that sounded like a good idea. "We will see what The Wise One thinks," he said.

He walked off to find The Wise One and ask his advice. Talks With The Animals was sure he had convinced his father that The Longnosed One would be very useful to them.

He was so confident that he decided to give the baby Longnosed One a name. Deer Pawn came up and asked if she could pet the baby Longnosed One. "I think he is still a little to afraid right now, let him get use to us first, then we will see. In the meantime we need to find a name for him.

It has to be a special name. A name that no one has ever had before. A few minutes later his father returned and said The Wise One told him that keeping the baby Longnosed One was a decision that Fights With The Bear and Talks With The Animals would have to decide for themselves. Whatever the decision they were responsible to do the right thing for the clan. "We'll sleep on it and decide in the morning."

Fights With The Bear talked with his wife Deer Eyes late into the night. He told her that Talks With The Animals wanted to keep the baby Longnosed One. "Somehow the baby Longnosed One seems to trust him. I guess our son really can talk to the animals. I think Talks With The Animals is right when he says that the baby Longnosed One will be a big help to the clan." Deer eyes replied, "If you really feel that way then there is nothing to decide, the baby Longnosed One is now part of the clan."

Talks With The Animals awoke early and rushed over to where he had left the baby Longnosed One the night before.

He had dreamed about the future; with him and the baby Longnosed One being almost inseparable. He knew that the dream would come true, it simply had too.

Chapter 5: The Baby Longnosed One becomes part of the Clan.

"I had a dream about us last night," Talks With The Animals said as he rubbed the baby Longnosed One's ears.

The baby Longnosed One seemed to be content with him as if it knew they were meant to be together. "We became partners, and I even dreamed of a name for you. It is a special name, it means brother, and it fits you. For you will be more than a companion, you will be like a brother to me. From now on you will be known as Sabe."

Fights With The Bear found his son with the baby Longnosed One.

"You can keep the baby Longnosed One for a while to see how it works out. If any problems arise we will have let him go, do you understand this?"

"Yes Father, I understand," Talks With The Animals said.

"I have given him a name, it is Sabe." "You must leave him for now. We have much work to do before we can move on."

Time went by quickly as the women smoked and packed meat in bundles to be carried by each member of the clan. Even the children would be required to carry a small pack. There was even a double pack for the baby Longnosed One to carry. They did not know when they might see meat again so they would carry as much as possible with them.

The warriors had spent the time fashioning tools from the bones of the Longnosed One. They had also made new spears from the white rock found along a stream bank nearby.

They would take the white rock and break off several hand size pieces first. Then they would take the smaller pieces and use a piece of deer antler to break off smaller and smaller pieces until the rock was transformed into an arrow point or knife.

What they needed now was skins to make clothes with. Now that they had enough meat to feed the clan for a whole moon they could worry about staying warm. But making clothes would have to wait for a few days. Fights With The Bear was very tired. He decided they needed to rest for one day before moving again. They had hauled all of the dead wood within several hundred yards of camp to smoke the meat from the Longnosed One. But they still had enough firewood left to last tonight. Tomorrow morning then, they would rest today and break camp in the morning.

The women could also use a rest. They had worked from sunup to sundown to get the meat prepared. His woman, Deer Eyes, had been covered in blood up to her shoulders trying to get at all the meat inside the carcass. She needed rest just as much as he did.

The next morning dawned clear and cool. It was getting on into new growing season, but it was still cold in the great hills. "Well, we'll see what you are going to do with that Longnosed One now that it is time to move on," The Lazy One sneered. Fights With The Bear Ignored him and went to see about getting everyone packed and ready to go. He found Talks With The Animals standing next to Sabe. Sabe was already wearing the pack prepared for him. "How did you get the pack on him?" he asked.

"Sabe used his long nose to help lift the pack up," Talks With The Animals said. "I told you Sabe would do what I asked him to." Fights With The Bear was impressed; his son must have some kind of magic spirit that allowed him to be brothers with the wild animals.

A little while later everyone was ready to go and the clan started their journey again. For some reason The Wise One insisted that they travel east instead of south. That was OK with Fights With The Bear. He was not sure but he thought The Wise One must have been visited by a spirit while sleeping. They walked all day; it was a very rough day. They had taken the whole day just to walk around one of the great hills, only to see a larger one directly in their path. They would have to go over the top of this hill.

Well, they weren't going any farther today. He could hear running water close by. Just ahead on the left was a great slab of gray rock that was nearly flat. "We will camp here for the night," he spoke loudly so everyone would hear.

Their clan had only forty-three members, ten of which were children. They could not risk losing any members due to careless mistakes caused by exhaustion.

Fights With The Bear sought out The Wise One. He had been giving commands without consulting him lately. He did not want to upset The Wise One by doing things that only The Wise One should do. He finally found The Wise One coming up the trail. The Wise One had fallen behind and was the last one to get to the camp site. Fights With The Bear realized with a shock that The Wise One looked very old and frail. The Wise One was breathing heavily and was stooped over. He appeared to be struggling with his small backpack. He had been The Wise One for as long as Fights With The Bear could remember. "Please forgive me for making decisions without talking with you first."

"But Fights With The Bear, you have talked with me every time you needed to. There are ways of talking without speaking." The Wise One replied. "Come and sit with me. There are things that I must tell you." Fights With The Bear sat on a large rock next The Wise One.

"My time has come. I am a very old man. I can no longer hunt for meat. It is time that I gave the position of The Wise One to a younger man who is capable of leading the clan in all things. That man is you, Fights With The Bear. You are a great warrior and a great leader.

"I will choose a place soon where I will die. It will be on top of the great hill that we must climb tomorrow. Once we reach the top of the great hill we will gather the clan and I will tell all that I have chosen you to take my place as The Wise One. I have talked to the spirits and they say it must be so.

Fights With The Bear arose early the next morning. He needed to be alone to think. He told Square Jaw that he would be back soon and set off into the woods. He was not worried about getting the people on the move this morning. Square Jaw knew what had to be done and he was a good leader.

They were settled down into a regular routine and did not need his assistance to strike camp and start the arduous climb up the great hill. He could easily catch up with them before they reached the top.

He would be carrying a huge responsibility if he was going to be The Wise One. He was not sure if he was the one for the job. Maybe it should be Square Jaw.

Square Jaw was a great warrior and he was always fair to everyone. He always did his part and more without ever complaining. Everyone valued his opinion, even The Wise One would ask for Square Jaw's opinion when making important decisions.

However, The Wise One had chosen him, and he would honor The Wise One's wishes. Suddenly Fights With The Bear thought of his own father. His father had been a great warrior in his time. He had even saved The Wise One's life once.

They were hunting the Longnosed Ones and had managed to trap one in a small waterhole. They had charged the Longnosed One before it could get out of the water. While they were in the middle of the attack the rest of the herd came tearing out of the woods into the clearing. The Wise One was the closest warrior and the leader had grabbed him up in his long nose before anyone knew what was going on. The Lazy One was next to The Wise One but he dropped his spear and ran when he saw what was happening.

His father had already plunged his spear into the Long Nosed One that had been trapped in the water hole. When he saw that The Wise One was in danger he had grabbed The Lazy One's spear and charged the lead Longnosed One that held The Wise One. He ran right up under it and thrust the spear deep into the Longnosed One's belly. The Longnosed One bellowed with rage and pain and dropped The Wise One. As his father tried to get away another Longnosed One grabbed him and flung him through the air. He landed hard and injured his leg. By this time several more warriors had attacked the herd. Luckily the one that his father had speared was the leader of the pack. It turned and retreated into the woods with the rest of the herd close behind.

The Wise One was bruised up some but otherwise he was OK thanks to the quick action of Fights With The Bear's father. However his father had not been so fortunate. He would be laid up for months and would never completely get over the injuries that he received.

Two years later when the clan had been on the move he finally gave up and passed away. Soon after they found the cave where they had lived for many years. The cave where his mother had died soon after moving there and was the first one placed in the back of the cave. It was where he grew up and became a great warrior. It was where he had been smitten with Deer Pawn and took her as his woman. The next year Talks With The Animals was born.

Fights With The Bear had not wanted to leave the cave that had been his home for many years. But when Square Jaw's baby died because she had no milk to drink he knew they had to leave or all of them would starve to death. He kept wondering what happened to all the animals that lived around the cave. When they had first arrived at the cave there was wildlife everywhere he looked. The first few years had been a time of plenty and the clan had prospered. Many of the little ones had been born.

But after the first few years it had gotten a little harder to find meat each year. They had to walk farther and farther on every hunting trip to find food. Finally in the past year they were not able to get enough meat to last through the winter. Clan members started starving and dying. Square Jaw's daughter was the last to die before leaving the cave. Now that he thought about it, The Wise One had told him that the clan had to move every few years because of lack of food. Could it be because of the people? Could they be the reason the animals all seemed to disappear? Time was getting on, he had better be leaving if he was going to catch up with the clan.

Chapter 6: The Wise One leaves the Clan

The climb to the top of the great hill was progressing slowly. Fights With The Bear caught up with the clan by midday. The Wise One was struggling to keep up with the clan. He looked even worse today. Fights With The Bear took The Wise One's pack and added it to his own. When the clan stopped to rest at midday, Fights With The Bear called Square Jaw over to talk. "When we start climbing again I want you to keep an eye on The Wise One. He is very weak and may get left behind. I will go ahead of the clan and look for a good spot to spend the night. We will not have time to get down the great hill today. We will have to camp on the top tonight and go down in the morning." Square Jaw nodded his head in agreement.

"Look up by the great rock that is near the top. The easiest path seems to head toward there. I will wait for the clan there."

Fights With The Bear went over to where his mate and son were resting. "Talks With The Animals, you take care of your mama, you hear? I am going ahead to find a good camping place on top of the great hill. Square Jaw is still leading the clan today. I'll see you all tonight at the top of the hill."

Fights With The Bear nodded to his wife and turned away. He had to do more than just find a good camping place. He had to also find a place where The Wise One would be comfortable for as long as he lived on top of the great hill.

Fights With The Bear was breathing hard. He could look up and see the top of the great hill. It was only another hundred feet or so to the top. In some places the climb had been quite steep. The clan would have a very hard time getting to the top today. He had made it in just under three hours but it would take the clan all day. Finally with one last step up he made it to the top. He stopped in his tracks and stared spellbound. He had never seen anything like this before in his life. Before him lay a beautiful valley.

There was a ribbon of water running through the valley. There must be a good sized stream down there.

It must be must be a days walk across and two or three days walk long, he thought. Most of the valley was covered with forest. But there were some large areas that were open and covered with grass. There were many dark spots among the grass. Fights With The Bear quickly recognized these as The Bearded Ones even though the nearest animals were over a thousand feet below him. There were hundreds of The Bearded Ones here! He could even see the thick mangy hair on their heads. There were a few bulls with thick horns standing guard over the herd.

And there, at the edge of the clearing was a herd of ten or fifteen of the Longnosed Ones! This must be paradise, he thought. Just then he noticed movement a few hundred feet down from him. He thought it was a bear and decided to go and get a closer look. The Great Pawed Ones were dangerous animals, especially if it was a mother bear with cubs. He was sure this bear had just come out of hibernation and would be very hungry. It might not be safe to camp here if the bear stayed in this area. Being careful to stay downwind of the bear he slowly slipped as close as he dared.

Fights With The Bear could not believe his eyes. This was not a bear at all. Yet it was very large and hairy like a bear. It seemed to move very slowly for some reason.

It had claws that were even bigger than a bear, yet Fights With The Bear sensed that it was not as dangerous. However after seeing those huge claws he was not going to take any chances. Fights With The Bear decided that he had seen enough. Just as he stood up to leave the animal looked in his direction.

Fights With The Bear pulled his spear forward and made ready to do battle. But the creature just looked at him a few moments then went back to feeding. Fights With The Bear slowly backed away then turned and headed back to the top of the great hill. He still needed to find a place for The Wise One to stay. Fights With The Bear knew he had found their new home. He had never seen so many large animals at one time before. It looked like good times ahead. His clan would grow and prosper now, he was sure.

Just as Fights With The Bear reached the top of the great hill he noticed a huge rock overhang facing the valley. He went over to inspect it. It was maybe twenty feet wide and ten feet high. The clan could camp here for the night. He stepped under the overhang to see how deep it was.

The floor sloped uphill slightly toward the back while the ceiling sloped down to meet the floor some fifteen feet from the front entrance. It was only possible to stand in an upright position near the front of the overhang. At least it would provide shelter from the wind and rain. Water was seeping out of the ground near the back of the cave. Fights With The Bear went over and scraped the dirt away from the area where the water was coming from. In just a few minutes the depression that he had made filled with water and he drank until he was full.

If The Wise One really wanted to stay on top of the great hill this would be a good place. Not only was there a source of water in the overhang itself but there was also a much larger spring coming out of the great hill below where he had seen the strange creature that looked like a bear.

After going over the entire area under the overhang, Fights With The Bear decided to head back down to meet the clan and show them the easiest way to the top of the great hill. The way he had come was very steep in some areas. He had noticed a way that was not near as steep as the way he had come. He climbed up on a large rock outcrop to get a better view. After looking for a few minutes he caught movement well below him. The clan was a little over halfway up the great hill. If he hurried he could get down in time to show them the easier route. It was longer this way but it was much easier to climb since it was not so steep.

An hour later Fights With The Bear met the clan coming up the hill. Amazingly The Wise One was riding on the back of the baby Long Nosed One. Fights With The Bear did not understand how the Longnosed One could climb these great hills and carry such a load at the same time. These animals must be much more sure footed than he thought. Even so it would never be able to climb the great hill at the point where Fights With The Bear had gone up this morning. It was a good thing he had found a much easier way to get to the top or the Longnosed One would have to be left behind.

These animals were really much more at home in the lower flood plains than they were in these great hills.

Even though the Long Nosed One was only a few years old it was already shoulder high and weighed much more than a human did. When full grown it would stand over eleven feet tall and weigh more than all forty-three people in the clan combined.

The clan members all sat down to rest while Fights With The Bear talked with Square Jaw. After eating some of the dried meat and resting for a while they started the climb gain. Two hours later they finally reached the top of the great hill. Fights With The Bear led them to the great overhang that he had found earlier. Several of the men set out to find wood for the cook-fires for the night, while the women began setting up camp.

After everyone had eaten and rested The Wise One rose and spoke loudly. "Please everyone come and join me around my fire. I wish to speak to the clan. Everyone please listen, for this is the last time that I will speak to the clan."

At this there was a great deal of whispering and murmuring. "Please everyone, be quiet and let me speak. I am an old man, my mate died many years ago. I have no living children. My body is no longer capable of keeping up with the demands that life imposes on it. I have decided that I will stay here on top of the great hill. I am ready to go to the next world where I will no longer be a part of this world. When the clan leaves to go down in the valley I will remain behind."

Now everyone began shouting, "But what will we do, who will lead us?"

The Wise One raised his hands for silence. You have many great warriors among you that are capable of being leaders. For instance, Square Jaw is a great warrior and very wise. He is very level headed and knows how to make the right decision. But there is one among you who is even a greater warrior and a better leader than Square Jaw. And he is the one that I have chosen to take my place. From this time forward, Fights With The Bear will be known as The Wise One.

At this The Lazy One jumped up and shouted, "How can you choose him, I am older and wiser than Fights With The Bear. I should be our clan's new leader."

The Wise One quietly responded, "You were not chosen for the very reason that you are speaking now. You do not show respect for others and you do not know how to lead. You only want to have everything your way. It takes a good follower to make a good leader. You will never be a leader until you learn to work with others and respect other people's wishes.

I have made my choice. Fights With The Bear, will you accept this position?"

Fights With The Bear stood and joined The Wise One in the center of the clan. "Yes, I will accept this position. I only hope that I can be as good a leader as you are."

"But, Fights With The Bear you are already a better leader than I was," The Wise One responded. I charge you with the safety and well being of this clan. I have spoken, from this day forward you will be known as The Wise One. Please come with me now for there are things which you must know.

"We are new to this land. When my great grandfather was just a child in the far-away land his clan ran out of food. All of the animals that were used for food went away, and the clan began starving. No one knew why the animals went away but I suspect that they were hunted and killed until there were none left.

"There were many many more people than we have in our clan. It was decided that the clan would split up into smaller groups. Part of the clan would stay behind. Some of the smaller groups would go to the land that rose out of the sea.

"My great grandfather was the leader of one of those groups that set off into the new land. Our clan has been on the move ever since. We will settle in a place for a while only to have to move again in a few years because of a lack of food. I have never seen or heard any of the other clans but I am sure that one day we will meet another clan."

Chapter 7: Life in the Great Valley

Fights With The Bear was happy and sad at the same time. He was now The Wise One and Square Jaw had taken over his duties as the chief warrior. In the future it would be Square Jaw leading the hunt. He could still participate in the hunt but it was Square Jaw that had to take the risks. Now that Fights With The Bear was The Wise One he was considered too valuable to risk being injured or killed during the hunt. It was going to take some getting used to, being The Wise One.

They had only been in the valley for a few weeks now and already the clan was doing much better. Two of the women were with child. Soon there would be little ones in the clan.

No one had spoken about The Wise One that had stayed on top of the great hill. He wondered for the hundredth time if the wise one was still alive. They had left him two full packs of dried meat. In addition there were now berries and other foods growing that could be eaten. The hot season was fast approaching.

Suddenly, his thoughts were interrupted by loud shouts and a lot of goings on in front of him. The men were on a hunt and he had stayed at the rear as was the custom of The Wise One. He quickly climbed to his feet and went to see what was going on. He was just in time to see a herd of Longnosed Ones stampede away from the waterhole where just a few moments before they had been peacefully lolling around.

The Lazy One fell to the ground and began thrashing around wildly. His hair was on fire, and he was shouting and beating at his own head furiously trying to put it out. Just then Square Jaw ran up and quickly laid right across The Lazy One's head and smothered the fire out.

The Lazy One bounded to his feet and began screaming at Talks With The Animals. However Square Jaw held him back so he could not get to Talks With The Animals. The Wise One demanded to know why The Lazy One was so upset with Talks

With The animals. It took several minutes for The Lazy One to calm down enough to speak without shouting.

Finally The Lazy One said, "You want to know why I am mad, I'll tell you why I am mad. That idiot son of yours just set my hair on fire. Not only that, we have lost the whole herd of Longnosed Ones because of it. Now we will have to start the hunt all over again."

Just then they heard the herd of Longnosed Ones start bellowing as if they were frightened and in pain. Everyone begin talking excitedly, what was making The Longnosed Ones bellow like they were? It was decided that they would send a scouting party up ahead and see what was going on. Square Jaw chose two warriors to accompany him and took off at a fast trot to see what was going on.

The Wise One asked Talks With The Animals if he had really set The Lazy One's hair on fire. "Yes Father, it is my fault. I was kneeling beside The Lazy One holding the fire stick. I must have let it get to close to The Lazy One's hair in all the excitement and it set his hair on fire."

Talks With The Animals hung his head in shame. How could he let such a thing happen, he would never be a great warrior like his father, who was now The Wise One. "Talks With The Animals, you owe The Lazy One an apology for what you have done."

"He owes me more than that, look at my head, I have no hair left."

"It is unfortunate that you lost most of your hair. Just be thankful that you did not get seriously burned," The Wise One responded. "I will hear no more complaints from you, Lazy One. If you had been ahead with the other warriors instead of hanging back with the women and children this would not have happened in the first place."

Just then one of the warriors that went with Square Jaw came into the clearing at a run. Shortly he drew up in front of The Wise One. "The Longnosed Ones are dead," he gasped. "All but two or three members ran right off a cliff just a short ways away. Apparently they were so frightened by the sight of The Lazy One thrashing around and yelling because his head was on fire that they stampeded right off the cliff. Square Jaw says to send everyone up immediately. There is more meat than the clan has ever seen at one time before!"

The Wise One called for everyone to follow and the whole clan took off after him. Just a few minutes later The Wise One saw a sight that thrilled and saddened him at the same time. There must be fifteen dead and dying Longnosed Ones lying at the base of a cliff some fifty feet below him.

So much meat! More meat than the whole clan could ever use.

Talks With The Animals had accidentally provided the Whole clan with meat enough to last the whole warm season. However Talks With The Animals was very sad. Because of him all of these animals were dead. What would Sabe think if he could understand what he had done? It was a good thing that he was still at their permanent camp instead of here on the hunt.

"Okay everyone, let's get busy, we have a lot of work ahead of us." The Wise One shouted. "We will prepare and smoke all of the meat that we can before it spoils. It will take days to get it done and hauled back to the main camp.

Talks With The Animals, bring your fire stick over here and get a fire going. We need all warriors to stand guard, with this much meat in one place there will be many dangerous animals drawn to the area. We must make all of the smoked meat we can." With this everyone began working hurriedly.

The women set to work on the carcasses cutting out meat strips to be dried over the camp fires. The children began gathering firewood. The only two old men in the clan put their knowledge to use making tools from the bones. They also made extra knives for the women. The whole camp was in a frenzy for the rest of the day.

Slowly things began to settle down as the excitement wore off and people grew tired. The Wise One realized there was too much to do all at once. He walked around and sent most of the women and children to bed. He went to Square Jaw and told him to send in half of his warriors to sleep and leave the rest on guard. For the next four days the entire clan stayed busy making smoked meat and tools for future use.

Yes, times are good, The Wise One thought to himself. It had been almost two moons since The Longnosed ones had ran off the cliff. The whole clan had to work feverishly to smoke meat but it was done now. After hauling the meat back to their permanent camp, everyone had gorged themselves and celebrated for several days afterwards. They now had enough smoked meat to make it through the next cold season with no problems.

After the great celebration was over they had gone back to work. But it was now much slower paced and there was much more free time to play games and hold tribal councils. Talks With The Animals had been immediately forgiven by everyone for spoiling the hunt when they saw what happened because of The Lazy One's hair catching on fire and stampeding The Longnosed Ones. Even The Lazy One had seemed to forget about it. However he would be changed for life, since when his hair finally grew out again it was short and frilly. He would never have the long flowing hair of a warrior again.

Yes, The Wise One thought, life is good. They had found a very nice cave that was just a couple hundred feet up the side of one the great hills that surrounded the valley. It was easy for the clan members to get to, and it afforded protection from outdoors and the wildlife in the area. The Great Toothed Cats had been seen in the valley, but so far none had come in close contact with any clan members.

Many of the women were with child now. Soon there would be lots of little ones in the clan. The Wise One had noticed lately that Talks With The Animals had been spending more and more time with Square Jaw's daughter and less time with Sabe. In a few more years perhaps Talks With The Animals would take Deer Pawn as his mate. The Wise One hoped so, it would be good to have many children in the tribe again. Even his own mate Deer Eyes was with child again. This pleased The Wise One greatly.

"Shall we hunt tomorrow, Wise One?" The Wise One's thoughts were interrupted by Square Jaw.

Yes, my friend we go on the hunt tomorrow. The clan had plenty of smoked meat, but they still needed clothing and other

40

items that the thick skin of The Longnosed One was not suitable for. There were several small herds of The Bearded Ones in the valley along with White Tails and many small game animals. The skin of The Bearded Ones would be worked into clothing for the long, cold months ahead.

The Wise One had come up with an idea based on what he had seen The Longnosed Ones do at the sight of fire. One of the small buffalo herds was in the habit of using the same watering hole that The Longnosed Ones used the day that they had been stampeded into running off the cliff.

The warriors would sneak into hiding places around the watering hole. Each would have a fire stick and a bundle of dried grass. When the herd arrived at the water hole and started drinking their fill, he would give the signal. Some of the warriors would light their bundles of grass and run toward the herd whooping and waving the burning grass. Other warriors would be hiding in strategic places and would show themselves at the right time to guide the stampeding animals right off the same cliff again. It was a good plan, but would it work? He would find out tomorrow.

"Square Jaw, be sure to go over my plan again with all of the warriors to make sure everyone knows what he is to do." The Wise One said. "Okay, when you see me take up my position you will know that everyone is in position and ready." Square Jaw responded. With this Square Jaw was off to make sure that everyone knew what to do.

The Wise One settled back and relaxed. They were in for a long wait. It was only mid-day and The Bearded Ones would not come to drink until sometime late that evening.

But The Wise One was not taking any chances, he wanted everyone in place and ready long before The Bearded Ones showed up. He did not want to take a chance on someone still moving around and spooking The Bearded Ones away before they reached the water hole.

Presently he saw Square Jaw signal that he was in position and all was well. All the preparations were done, all they could do now was wait and see if his plan would work.

Finally he saw the herd. They were still a good five minutes of fast walking away. They were slowly browsing their way toward the water hole. The Wise One waited patiently for them to arrive at the water hole. It would still be another half hour or so before they arrived at the water hole. The Wise One hoped everyone else could wait and not move before he gave the signal. They had all been instructed not to do anything until he gave the signal.

Finally the herd stopped eating and as if on signal they all began marching straight to the water hole. The Wise One's heartbeat speeded up. It was now or never. Most of the herd was at the water hole now. As soon as the last two or three arrived and lowered their head to drink he would give the signal.

Suddenly someone moved, it was The Lazy One, he must have grown impatient. But the last Bearded One had not lowered his head yet. It caught the movement and sounded the alarm. The entire herd immediately turned and bolted back the way that they had come. However The Wise One was already giving the signal. He lit his own grass bundle and ran forward to try and turn the herd. The other warriors followed his example.

Suddenly from The Wise One's right, The baby Longnosed one came crashing out of hiding with Talks With The Animals riding on his back. The sight of The Long Nosed One plus all the warriors running at them with burning grass caused mass panic and confusion in the herd. It split in two with one section turning again while the rest thundered away down the path they had come to the water hole on. One of the warriors was standing directly in their path. He realized what was happening and made a desperate lunge for cover.

He did not react quickly enough. Just as he turned to jump clear the lead Bearded Ones horn caught him in the side and he was immediately dragged to the ground in front of the onrushing herd. He never had a chance.

Meanwhile, the rest of the herd had turned and was headed in the general direction of the cliff. Talks With The Animals urged The Longnosed One after the herd while the other warriors fell in behind to give chase. The herd was slowly veering off course, but the warrior who been stationed to help guide the herd showed himself. He waved the burning straw wildly and screamed at the top of his lungs. It worked, the herd was turned back slightly. They missed the warrior by just inches and were now rushing headlong for the cliff. The leader saw the land give away at the cliff and tried to stop. However he was immediately swept on from behind by the herd in their mad attempt to get away from the terrible moving screaming, fire-toting warriors. The whole herd ran blindly off the cliff in their panic.

The Longnosed One came to a stop and Talks With The Animals jumped to the ground and ran over to the cliff. He was soon joined by the other warriors. The warriors starting giving war whoops and cheers on seeing all the animals at the bottom of the cliff. The hunt had been a success. Even though The Lazy One had jumped up too early and spooked the herd, they still had managed to drive over half of the herd over the cliff. Talks With The Animals did not feel so happy. He knew that his tribe would perish without warm cloths. But he still felt sick to the stomach at the sight of all the dead animals that he had just helped destroy. He went back to where he had left The Longnosed One. Sabe was stamping his feet and snorting loudly. "What is the matter, Sabe? Does all this commotion make you nervous?" he asked. He began to speak softly to Sabe to calm him down. "I know how you feel Sabe, it upsets me also. Come we will leave this place."

"Can I have everyone's attention please, I have a very important announcement to make." It was Square Jaw speaking.

"Tonight we welcome another warrior. We have one who has come of age. He has proved his worth on the hunt. Everyone has heard how Talks With The Animals and Sabe saved the day by turning the stampeding herd back toward the cliff. From this day forward Talks With The Animals is a full warrior. He will no longer be required to do child's labor. He is now a warrior for our clan. He will be treated with the respect that all our other warriors receive."

"But he is not fully grown yet," The Lazy One objected. "He is younger than my brother's son by a full year."

"It does not matter," Square Jaw replied. Talks With The Animals has proven that he is a warrior by his actions on the hunt. I am the head warrior and I say that Talks With The

Animals is now a warrior. The only one who can stop this from happening is The Wise One."

At this all eyes turned to The Wise One. "Square Jaw has spoken, so it will be." The Wise One said. The Wise One's chest swelled with pride. His son was now a warrior. It seemed like it was just yesterday that he had been bouncing Talks With The Animals on his knee. Now he was a warrior.

Young he may be, but he had proven to be valuable to the clan.

The Wise One felt much more comfortable with Talks With The Animals taking Sabe on the hunt now. He had given his permission for Talks With The Animals to take Sabe along with some consternation on his part. What if Sabe panicked and alerted the herd or even worse trampled one of the warriors during the hunt? It would have been The Wise One's burden because he had given permission for Sabe to be used on the hunt. But The Longnosed One had proved his worth on the hunt. Their clan only had a little over a dozen warriors.

With one recently killed on the hunt, Talks With The Animals and Sabe would be sorely needed, even in this valley of plenty.

Even while The Wise One was having all these thoughts his facial expression did not change. He was The Wise One, and the whole clan depended on him to be level headed at all times, no matter what may being going on around him. He must be calm and make the right decision or the clan might suffer or even perish.

He still secretly thought of himself as Fights With The Bear. He had been called Fights With The Bear for many years.

It was a good name and he had earned it the hard way. He was only about nineteen years old at the time. The clan had just come through a long, cold, harsh winter. The growing season was just beginning. Once again the clan was on the brink of starvation. Their winter food stores were all but gone and there just was not any animals around to be killed for meat. The clan had decided to send out several small hunting parties. Each party would take off in a different direction and walk for two full days

44

to try and find animals to hunt. It was hoped that by covering a larger area they would have a better chance finding meat.

After traveling for two days Fights With The Bear and his hunting partner, Square Jaw, were caught in a late winter snowstorm. They started looking for a place to wait out the storm. After looking for hours they finally found a small cave. They immediately split up and went off to find enough firewood to last out the storm. Fights With The Bear returned first and crawled into the cave. The opening was too low to walk into. After crawling just a few feet the cave opened up into a great room.

Just as he laid down his armload of firewood something hit him a terrific blow on his left shoulder. The blow knocked him to the floor and numbed his left arm, he could already feel blood oozing out of his arm. Then he heard a loud roar and realized that he had crawled into a cave with a bear in it. He quickly pulled out his stone hunting knife.

There was just enough light for him to see the entrance that he had crawled through. There was only one problem; the bear was between him and the entrance. The bear stood upright and charged him. He charged the bear and lunged his stone knife into the bear's neck with all his might. It did not stop the bear, it grabbed him and they fell to the floor with the bear on top. The wind was knocked out of Fights With The Bear, but at the same time when the bear fell the stone knife struck the floor and was driven all the way up to the handle in the bears neck. Luckily it severed the bear's jugular vein. The bear died almost instantly. Fights With The Bear lay pinned under the bear until his hunting partner returned several minutes later. His arm was cut badly and the bleeding needed to be stopped or he would bleed to death.

Faintly he heard Square Jaw call out, "Hey, where are you? Have you already gone into the cave?"

"Here, I'm inside," Fights With The Bear croaked out. Finally he heard his hunting partner crawling through the entrance. "I'm over here," he called again. "Help me, I was attacked by a bear. I think it's dead, I think I killed it."

"Where is it? I don't see it anywhere," Square jaw quickly replied.

"It's lying on top of me, get it off."

Square Jaw's eyes finally adjusted enough to the low light of the cave to see them. He grabbed the bear by the hind leg and tried to drag it off, but the bear was to heavy.

"You will have to roll it off, it's to heavy to drag."

Between the two of them they were able to roll the bear enough for Fights With The Bear to get free.

Square Jaw went to work to stop the bleeding and to make him comfortable. Fights With The Bear had passed out soon afterwards and did not wake up until the next day. He felt much better than expected when he finally awoke. His arm was swollen and stiff, but he was sure that with a few days rest he would be Okay. Square Jaw skinned the bear and began smoking the meat. They would eat all that they could hold and carry the remainder back to the clan. The snow had stopped falling and there was only six inches or so on the ground. After spending two more nights in the small cave Fights With The Bear felt that he was well enough to travel.

They tied the smoked meat up into packs and headed back to the clan. With their heavy loads they had to stop and rest so often that it took them almost four days to get back.

The other hunting parties had even worse luck than they did. Only one White Tail and a few long ears had been killed. There just wasn't any animals around anymore.

However, with the meat from the bear the clan managed to hold on until the warm season returned. After Square Jaw told how the bear was killed, Fights With The Bear was given his present name.

The whole clan thought that Fights With The Bear was the greatest warrior of all after this. The story was told many times with Fights With The Bear becoming more powerful with each telling.

Fights With The Bear knew that it had been luck more than fighting skill that saved him that day. If the bear had not fallen and driven the knife deep into it's throat then Fights With The Bear would be dead now. But no one wanted to hear this; he had killed a bear with only a knife for a weapon.

But now he was no longer Fights With The Bear, he was The

Wise One. To him The Wise One would always be the old man he had left on the great hill when entering the valley.

He wondered if the old man was still alive. He had the urge again to climb the great hill and see. However he had been told by The Wise One before him that the place was sacred and no one could come their unless it was to die. And so it would be.

Chapter 8: Talks With The Animals leaves the Clan

"This is not fair," The Lazy One complained. "You are getting all of the best grapes." You can reach much higher with that Longnosed One's help. Maybe you should stand on the ground like everyone else so we will all have a chance of getting some." The Lazy One was mad because Talks With The Animals could reach much higher while standing on the back of Sabe. Not only this, but Sabe would grab a hold to a vine and pull so hard that the trees would bend down and reveal many more grapes.

It was a warm autumn afternoon and most of the clan was out foraging for the grapes. They had been in this valley for well over two years now. The warm season was fast giving way to the cold season. But for the first time the clan members were not worried. The food was still very plentiful here in the valley. Since they had learned how to drive animals over a cliff using fire they had not gone hungry again, even during the coldest weather.

The clan was slowly finding more and more uses for the plants growing in the great valley. Not only were some of them good to eat, but plants had many other uses also. The grapes were a favorite treat of the clan. They grew on vines that grew in the lower areas along the many streams of the great valley. The vines twisted in and out among the branches of the great trees growing there.

"I'll tell you what I'll do," Talks With The Animals called down to The Lazy One. "I'll get Sabe to pull one of the vines down so you can reach the grapes. "He whispered into Sabe's ear and then Sabe proceeded to pull down very hard on the vine where The Lazy One was standing. Finally the tree bent over far enough for The Lazy one to reach the vines. "Grab a hold of the vine so Sabe can let go," he instructed The Lazy One.

"Okay I've got it," The Lazy One responded.

As soon as Sabe let go of the tree, it immediately stood back upright, pulling the vine violently out of The Lazy One's hands. In the process it rubbed across The Lazy One's face crushing grapes against it. His face turned purple from the juice of the grapes. The Lazy One bellowed in pain, "You did that on purpose, I'll get you for that."

But Sabe raised his trunk and roared a challenge that quickly changed The Lazy One's mind.

Talks With The Animals responded, "No, I did not do that on purpose. I thought you had a good hold on the vine."

"Well I was not ready, you let it go to soon," The Lazy One replied."

"Okay, I'll get Sabe to pull it down for you again, this time be ready to hold to it when Sabe lets go. Sabe reached up and pulled the vine down again and held it. The Lazy One grabbed a hold with both hands and braced himself.

"Okay, you can let it go now, I have it," The Lazy One called. Sabe let it go again.

The tree straightened up again, only this time The Lazy One was gripping the vine tightly with both hands. When the tree straightened up it pulled The Lazy One off his feet and swung him through the air to land in the middle of the creek twenty feet away. He landed with a big splash, but was not seriously hurt since the water broke his fall. He jumped to his feet screaming like a mad man and shaking his fist at Talks To The Animals. The whole clan began laughing hysterically at The Lazy One, which made him even more furious. However one look at Sabe was enough to calm him down. He took off at a fast walk mumbling to himself.

Everyone began feeding on the luscious grapes again. It had been very entertaining for all but The Lazy One.

Talks With The Animals was happy. He had Sabe, who was the greatest friend he could ask for. He had a baby sister only a few moons old. And then there was Square Jaw's daughter, Deer Pawn. Every time he saw her she looked even more beautiful. He would save a whole pouch full of the grapes and take them with him when he went to visit their camp tonight. They were staying in one of the new shelters that the clan had recently learned how to make since living in the valley. It had been Talks With The Animals who came up with the idea of making the moveable shelters.

The clan was doing well. Already, half a dozen children had been born since they had settled in the great valley.

The cave was not big enough to house all of the clan members anymore. The women who had babies and little ones wanted more privacy than what could be had in the cave. This was all new to Talks With The Animals. Always in the past the clan had stayed together in the same cave or whatever shelter they could find.

But since moving into the great valley things were beginning to change. They had killed so many of the bearded ones that they had more skins than they needed for clothes. Talks With The Animals Father had hung several of the skins over some small bushes to save and use at a later date.

The next day his father wanted one of the skins that he had hanging over the bushes. He was going to make one more overcoat as a spare since cold weather would soon be here.

He asked Talks With The Animals to go and fetch one of the skins for him. As Talks With The Animals picked up one of the skins he noticed that the bushes and ground were dry where the skin had been. The significance of this did not dawn on him until a couple of days later. He was sitting and talking to Deer Pawn who was keeping an eye on several of the little ones when he noticed that two small girls were under one the skins playing like they were taking care of a baby. He suddenly remembered how dry it had been under the skin when he had picked it up the other day for his father. If they could figure out a way to prop up the skins they would have a dry place to stay that could be taken anywhere that they went.

He went to talk to his father about this immediately. I will see you later, Deer Pawn, I must go and find my father and talk to him." He set off to find his father.

His father was now The Wise One and was always helping out other families in the clan. He found his mother, Deer Eyes, and asked her where his father might be. "He has gone to see The Lazy One's family. The Lazy One is having a dispute with

51

one of his brothers and The Wise One was asked to come and settle it for them." She responded. "They are down near the creek where you keep Sabe."

Talks With The Animals finally found his father but had to wait for another half hour to speak with him. "Father, I have a good idea. I know what we can do with all of the skins that we have leftover. We can make a temporary shelter out of them. Just think, when we go on the hunt we will be able to stay dry even in the hardest rain.

"Remember the other day when you sent me out to bring you one of the extra skins. It had been raining hard the night before, yet when I picked up the skin, the bushes and ground were dry where it had been laying. If we could figure out a way to hold the skins together we will have a shelter to keep us dry anywhere we go. We will no longer be cold and miserable when it rains.

The Wise One thought about it for a few minutes and could not find fault with the idea. "It is a good idea, tomorrow we will try to see if we can make a shelter."

The next day The Wise One gathered the clan together and told of Talks With The Animal's idea. Everyone agreed that it was worth a try. The warriors broke up into several groups. Each one took several skins and proceeded to try and make a shelter out of the skins. After trying for hours no one had come up with a way to hold up the skins so a person could get under them without having to hold them up.

Finally The Wise One had an idea. "Listen, I think I know a way it can be done," he called. "We will make a frame similar to what we use to smoke meat over a fire, only it will have to be much bigger. We will need to find some small trees and cut them down. We will need poles at least twice as tall as I am and they must be straight. All of the warriors set off to find trees that could me made into poles like The Wise One described. By the time they found enough poles to work with it was too late in the day to continue.

The next morning the whole clan gathered and started trying to stack the poles together. However, after standing the poles up and leaning them together where they touched at the top end, they discovered that no one was tall enough to lash them together where they leaned against each other.

"We will have to lash them together and then stand them up all at one time," The Wise One said. After lashing them together they found that two people could stand the poles upright. Once they were standing straight up, one person could hold them while another grabbed one pole at the time and spread them out at the bottom. Now the problem was, with the poles up they were to high and big to be covered with skins. Deer Pawn suggested that they sew the skins together to make one big skin that would be big enough.

Another day went into sewing the skins together. Finally they were ready to try again. "Let's lash one end of the skins to the top end of the poles before we stand them up right," The Wise One directed. "Then after the poles are up we can just drag the skins around and around until we have covered the whole frame." After several hours of trial and error they finally succeeded in making a reasonably good shelter.

Several of the families in the clan had made a shelter and were now living in them, including Talks With The Animal's family. This had opened up space in the cave for the remaining clan members. As a result there was much less tension and everyone seemed to be getting along much better.

Yes, Talks With The Animals thought to himself, things are going mighty well. He finally got his fill of the grapes. He proceeded to fill the two small pouches up with the sweet balls. He would give one pouch to his mother and carry the other one to Deer Pawn. Presently he had his bags full, but Sabe was still eating. He decided to leave Sabe, since the Longnosed One might spend several more hours eating. Sabe never strayed far from where the clan was, even when a herd of The Longnosed Ones were nearby.

Talks With The Animals returned to his family's shelter and gave one of the pouches of the grapes to his mother. She hugged him and told him how proud she was of him. He was going to be a great warrior just like his father was. He hung around the shelter for a while but finally he could take no more. He simply had to go and see Deer Pawn.

53

He told his mother that he would be back later; he was going over to Square Jaw's shelter to visit for awhile. His mother was not fooled. She knew that he was really going to see Deer Pawn. But that was okay with her. Deer Pawn was a very pretty young girl. She was also a very good worker even at her young age. She would make a good companion for Talks With The Animals.

Talks With The Animal's heart was in his throat. He had just arrived at Square Jaw's shelter. There sat Deer Pawn, and at the sight of her his heart had started pounding. He had never felt this way before. What was going on. Deer Pawn was the same girl that he had known and played games with all of his life. Why all of a sudden did she make him feel this way? He would have to speak to his father about this sometime.

"Here, Deer Pawn, I brought these for you," he managed to squeak out as he handed her the pouch full of grapes.

"Why thank you, Talks With The Animals," she said. "I will carry them to my mother, I'll be right back." Talks With The Animals was disappointed. It was as if she did not care if he was here or not. She took the pouch to her mother and told her that Talks With The Animals had brought them over.

Talks With The Animals wasn't sure what to do now. He did not understand women. He felt uncomfortable around them. Well I must think of something to impress her, he thought to himself. Just then The Lazy One's nephew, Swims Like A Fish arrived at Square Jaw's camp. Talks With The Animals knew he was here to see Deer Pawn.

Just after Swims Like A Fish arrived Deer Pawn came out of the shelter. She gave a small cry of surprise when she saw him. Swims Like A Fish grinned and spoke softly to her while pointing at Talks With The Animals. Then they both started laughing very loudly. Talks With The Animals felt sure that they were laughing at him. He abruptly turned and walked away. He heard Deer Pawn call after him, but that just made him walk even faster.

He went down to the clearing where Sabe usually stayed during the night. Sabe trumpeted loudly in greeting when he saw Talks With The Animals. Good old Sabe he was always happy to see him. Talks With The Animals knew exactly where he stood with Sabe. They seemed to be made for each other.

They made a great team. Sabe nudged him playfully and Talks With The Animals began to scratch behind his ears. It was as if he and Sabe could read each other's minds. He felt much closer to Sabe than to even his own father.

But still his mind seemed to be filled with thoughts of Deer Pawn all the time. But what could he do? If Swims Like A Fish was interested in her then surely he had no chance.

Swims Like A Fish was a year older than he was, and he always seemed to know the right things to say around Deer Pawn. It seemed like they were always talking and laughing together.

Swims Like A Fish was very tall and lean, and unlike his uncle, The Lazy One, he was fast becoming a good warrior. How could he compete with someone like that?

"Well Sabe, I guess it's just you and me like always," he spoke out loud. Suddenly an idea occurred to Talks With The Animals. He was coming of age. Most young warriors usually went off and lived for a time by themselves before taking a woman. If Deer Pawn had no interest in him then he just as well go off exploring like he had dreamed of doing many times. Only now he was really not so sure that he wanted to go. Maybe he should stay here and try to win Deer Pawn's heart. But with Swims Like A Fish around all of the time, he never seemed to be able to get Deer Pawn alone long enough to let her know how he really felt about her. Well, he had made up his mind, he was going. He would talk to his father, The Wise One, and see what he thought.

The next day Talks With The Animals sought out The Wise one and told him his plans. "Now is not a good time to go, my son. Why don't you wait until you are a couple of years older?" his father urged. "Why don't you stay here through the cold season and go next year.

"But Father I can carry enough food with me to get me through the cold season. I have Sabe and he can carry a much bigger load than I could," he had argued.

It is true that Sabe can carry a great load even though he is only half grown. But you must remember that there will not be much food for The Long Nosed One to eat during the cold season. You must not work him to hard or he may not make it through the cold season."

"Yes, but the cold season is still two moons away, we will have time to find a place to hold up for the winter. And with all the extra skins we have I can make another shelter to take with me."

"Very well, son, if your mind is made up I will not try to dissuade you any longer. If you are going to go we must get busy and make another shelter for you. I will go get your mother to sew more skins together for a new shelter. You can go and gather poles for the frame. I will gather food and make up a pack for you."

So just three days after making the decision, Talks With The Animals bid farewell to his mother and father. Then he and Sabe were on their way. He had been so busy preparing for the trip that he did not see Deer Pawn to say goodbye. Well she was not interested in him anyway, she probably would not even know that he was gone. However, Talks With The Animals thoughts were just the opposite of what Deer Pawn felt.

When she found out that he had left without even saying goodbye to her she had ran to here mother and cried. "Oh Mother, what have I done? Maybe I went to far with Swims Like A Fish. I only talked and flirted with him to make Talks With The Animals jealous. I even told Swims Like A Fish that I could never love him for my heart was already taken by another. But Swims Like A Fish said that he would still try to win me over. If not, then he would still be my friend.

"Oh mother, what have I done?" she wailed again.

Her mother took Deer Pawn in her arms and held her. "Do not worry my child," she whispered. "He will return to you."

"But mother how can you be so sure."

"Because, dear child, I am old and wise and I know these things." "Did you ever tell Talks With The Animals how you felt about him?" she asked.

"No Mother, I did not, but surely he must know," Deer Pawn replied.

"Well when you see him again, do not take any chances. If you really love him then tell him so."

But by this time Talks With The Animals was already many miles away. He was not sure where he was going. By chance he started Sabe out heading south when he left the clan. Soon after leaving he jumped on Sabe's back and started dozing off. He really did not care where they went as long as it was away from the clan. He could not stand to see Deer Pawn with Swims Like A Fish anymore. His heart just could not take it. He hoped they would be happy together.

He let Sabe go where he wanted while he dozed off. Sabe walked for a while then stopped and pulled a few choice branches from the smaller trees to eat. They slowly traveled toward the southern end of the valley. Finally, just before dark, Talks With The Animals decided to camp for the night.

He had been riding Sabe all day. He spoke aloud to The Longnosed One, "We'll stop here for the night, Sabe. I know where we are at. There is a small stream just over at the edge of this clearing. I remember camping here once before when we were on the hunt." This is as far south as anyone in the clan had been before. They were heading to the southern end of the great valley. "I'm sorry I didn't keep you company today Sabe but I promise I will do better tomorrow. I will walk all day tomorrow and give you a break." Sabe trumpeted and knelt down so Talks With The Animals could get off.

Talks With The Animals quickly pulled the pack off Sabe and scratched him behind the ears. Sabe seemed to really enjoy that and would stand there as long as Talks With The Animals kept scratching. After a few minutes Talks With The Animals stopped scratching and sent Sabe off to eat. Sabe was so big that he had to spend hours every day eating in order to get enough.

Talks With The Animals took the coals that he had wrapped in green leaves and made a small fire. It's a good thing I stopped when I did he thought as he made a fire. In another hour the coals would have been completely out and he would have been without fire. There really should be a better way to keep fire; he would have to think of a better way one of these days. He was not cold, but he thought that a fire might cheer him up. He ate a meal of smoked meat and topped it off with some of the grapes that he liked so much.

· He thought of Deer Pawn again. Maybe he should have told her how he felt. But it was too late now. She was back at the clan flirting with Swims Like A Fish. There was nothing he could do about it now. Tomorrow he would be in new territory that no one in the clan had seen before. He would stay busy exploring so he would not think about Deer Pawn anymore.

It rained lightly during the night and Talks With The Animals awoke to a warm, muggy morning. He sat up and stretched, then set off to find Sabe. The Longnosed One would probably be up and grazing by now. He climbed up a small outcrop of boulders to get a better view. There were more trees here than there was further up the valley. He was just high enough to see above the trees surrounding him. He could see for miles back up the valley he had just come from. However, on each side and behind him were more of the great hills. So this was the southern end of the Great Valley. After looking at the beautiful view for a few minutes he spotted Sabe A few hundred feet away feeding quietly.

He could not see a way to go any further south without climbing over the great hills again. But he could just see the top of a hill over the trees that was not as high as the great hills at the southern end of the valley. If he could climb up that small hill he might get a better view and find a way to go without climbing the great hills again.

He decided it was worth a try. Sabe was feeding and would not go far. He looked carefully at the great hills around him to get his bearings before setting off to climb the hill.

Two hours later Talks With The Animals reached the top of the hill. The southern end of the valley appeared to be completely closed in by the great hills. He could see a river on the east side of the hill between him and the great hills in the distance. His eyes followed the river back toward the south. The river appeared to be coming right out of the southernmost portion of the valley.

Suddenly he had an idea. If the water could find a way through the great hills then all he had to do was follow the river south and he would not have to climb over the great hills. His mind was made up almost as soon as he had the idea. He would follow the river and see where it went. He would rest up today and let Sabe eat his fill. The way would be tough going for Sabe and he would need his strength.

He set off back to his camp. The sun was high in the sky now and he was getting hot. It seemed like the growing season was getting hotter every year. When he reached his camp he decided to build up his fire and have another good meal. He had several hours of daylight left yet. As he stirred around in the ashes he realized with a start that the fire had gone out! When he left camp this morning he had not built up the fire. He scratched desperately through the coals until he hit dirt. There was no fire left! When the cold season started he could freeze to death without fire for protection. How did he get himself into this mess anyway. He should have stayed in camp where he belonged. He was only one long days march away from camp. If he started out first thing in the morning he could be back with the clan by nightfall.

He dismissed that idea immediately. He had come out here alone to prove to himself that he was a man. He would not go back now. He would be the laughing stock of the whole clan if he came back after being gone just two days. Well, the warm season was still here; with luck there would not be any really cold nights for a couple of moons. Even though he had acquired a taste for cooked meat he had eaten raw meat before and could do so again.

All was not lost; he could make it without fire until the end of the warm season anyway. However, in the future he had better be more careful, for his next mistake might be his last. Tomorrow he would follow the river south through the great hills.

Talks With The Animals was up at dawn the next morning packing his few belongings. He went and found Sabe almost immediately. It was uncanny how Sabe seemed to be nearby at just the right time. Talks With The Animals loaded his skins on Sabe, shouldered his food pouch and spear and set off for the river. Since he was on the opposite side of the hill from the river

59

he headed directly south. The river flowed from the southwest to the northeast so he would intersect it a few miles south where the great valley ended and the great hills rose up to the sky.

After walking for a couple of hours he noticed a strange land formation. He could not see it clearly because of the ever-present trees in the area. He decided to go and investigate further. After all he was out exploring so he might as well make the most of it. He had several days supply of food left so he could take his time and learn his way around the country for now.

When he reached the outcropping of rocks he had seen earlier he was astonished at what he saw. There was a huge arc of rock with nothing under it, forming a natural bridge.

He had never seen anything like it before. This must be a sacred place. He must investigate it further. He decided to explore the local area today and take up his journey tomorrow. He could only imagine what he might find on this journey.

He climbed to the top of the arc and looked out over the great valley. No matter how many times he looked out over the valley it never ceased to amaze him with its beauty. He stood on top of the natural bridge for hours looking over the valley. He wanted to memorize what the valley looked like from this direction. He had learned to look behind while he was traveling. Looking at a scene in the opposite direction from which you travel through it could completely change how it looked. And he wanted to be able to come back this way when he was ready to return home. He could see many miles to the north, up the valley. He tried to find the spot in the valley where the clan was living but it was just too far away.

He wondered if he would ever see the clan again. Suddenly he felt very alone. He missed his parents. His father was now The Wise One and would be very busy taking care of the clan. Did his father miss him? Probably not, he was too busy to worry about his son going on a foolish journey.

Upon reaching the river he turned and began following it upstream. He hoped that river actually flowed all the way across the great hills and didn't just start on this side of them. Judging by the size of the stream it should be many miles to where it began.

After traveling all day he had only traveled a few miles up river. The going was much harder here than it had been in the valley floor. The river did not flow in a straight line but meandered back and forth in countless arcs. On top of this there were many large boulders in and around the river that made traveling even harder. He could manage pretty good but the going was especially difficult for Sabe. Sabe was growing bigger every day and it was becoming more and more difficult for him to move in the forest.

At nightfall, Talks With The Animals stopped to camp. He would have to find an easier route or he would be forced to turn back because of Sabe. He would never leave Sabe behind for any reason. Either they went together or they did not go at all. Sabe was like a brother to Talks With The Animals.

Talks With The Animals rested for a few minutes then got up and removed his pack from Sabe. For once Sabe did not appear to be hungry. He just stood there and let Talks With The Animals rub behind his ears. Talks With The Animals could see that Sabe was very tired. Maybe he pushed him too hard. He would have to take better care of Sabe in the future.

"I promise you I'll find an easier way tomorrow or we will turn back," he said softly to Sabe. "I am sorry that I did not look out for you better today. I will do my best to make it easier for you in the future." Sabe trumpeted as if he understood every word Talks With The Animals said.

"Well you can rest tonight and in the morning while I find a way through," he said. Talks With The Animals laid out his skins and was soon fast asleep.

He awoke the next morning to the sound of Sabe eating branches and leaves along the riverbank. They were still in extreme southern end of the great valley. There were great hills on either side of the river. There was another smaller hill similar to the one he had climbed the day before. Talks With The Animals decided to climb up the hill and get another view again.

From the top of the hill he could only see patches of the river. Most of it was hidden by trees. He could tell where the river was because the trees were much thicker and taller along its banks. Once you got away from the river the trees thinned out and in some places he could even see open spaces where The Bearded Ones roamed. He could even see a few of The Bearded Ones in one large clearing.

He could see the river winding back and forth. If he stayed back away from the river a ways and did not try to follow its every curve he would make much better time. Also the going would be easier because the trees were much farther apart away from the river.

Talks With The Animals descended from the hill and returned to his campsite. Sabe was still near the river feeding. It was amazing how much Sabe could eat in a single day.

Talks With The Animals estimated that Sabe could eat more limbs and leaves in one day than he could pick up with both arms.

"Okay Sabe, let's move on," Talks With The Animals called out as he returned to camp. Sabe grabbed one last limb full to eat and returned to Talks To The Animals. "Good old Sabe, you are always there when I need you," Talks With The Animals said as he rubbed Sabe behind the ears again.

Scratching Sabe tended to calm and please Talks With The Animals almost as much as it did Sabe, though he had never really thought about it before. Presently Talks With The Animals stooped down and got his pack and loaded it on Sabe's back. Then he picked up his food pouch and they were on their way again.

They made much better headway by paralleling the general course of the river rather than trying to follow its every bend. However, the way was still difficult for Sabe to follow and Talks With The Animals stopped frequently to let him rest. They had been steadily climbing all day. Several times it had appeared as if the great hills would block the way but the river had found a way through.

Finally in the late afternoon as they topped out on a small rise where two of the great hills almost met on either side of the river. Talks With The Animals saw another valley.

It was much smaller than the great valley that he had just left behind. At this point the river curved to the right and went along the back side of the great hill. Talks With The Animals took a few minutes to memorize the features of the hills around him.

The valley stretched out in the same general direction that he had been traveling for the last few days. He had to make up his mind where he wanted to go. Should he turn to the northeast and follow the river, or continue on the same way into the valley? Once again he scratched Sabe behind the ears as he contemplated his next move. He finally decided to follow the river on its new course.

"We will camp here for the night and move on in the morning," he said to Sabe. He had acquired the habit of talking to Sabe as if he were a person who understood his every word. Once again he set up camp for the night. Sabe moved off to the river's edge and began browsing again.

The next morning they set off up the river on their new course. Talks With The Animals suddenly came to a halt. Near the river only a few hundred feet away was a small herd of The Bearded Ones. They were all drinking quietly. If he could get close enough he might be able to kill one. He whispered to Sabe to stay, and slowly started advancing toward the herd. He kept as much cover between him and the herd as he could find. He would have to work quickly; in just a few minutes the herd would be finished drinking and wander off to feed. He got in place behind a small bush just as the herd started drifting away from the waterhole.

Since he no longer had fire he could not drive the herd where he wanted it. He would have to take a chance that they would come close enough for him to use his spear. He settled down to wait for the herd to come by. As he watched the herd he noticed that one old bull was limping pretty bad. If the herd did not come close enough then maybe he could run down the old bull and kill it. Finally the herd was close enough for him to try for a kill. There was a young calf that was running around and playing as his mother was feeding. If it kept circling around its mother it would pass within twenty feet of where he was. Forget the old bull, he was going to have a tender calf for super tonight.

He slowly raised his spear and made ready to throw it at the calf. Just a few more seconds and the calf would be in range.

Suddenly he heard a loud crashing sound behind him and Sabe began bellowing loudly. The entire herd turned as one and rushed off in a mad dash towards the woods along the river. He jumped up and chased after the calf but he was too late, the herd was rapidly leaving him behind. He broke off the pursuit and returned to where Sabe was waiting for him.

"What did you do that for?" he shouted angrily at Sabe.

"I had food for sure and you ruined it. Now I will have to go hungry and its all your fault. Maybe I should have let The Lazy One kill you that day long ago." Sabe hung his head and turned away. He did not understand all that Talks With The Animals said but he sure understood that he had upset his master. Talks With The Animals was immediately sorry for what he said. Just as he started to call out to Sabe to come back he saw something out of the corner of his eye.

He was standing close to the bush where he had been hiding while waiting for the calf to come into range of his spear. Just ten feet behind where he had been crouching were the footprints of the Long Toothed One. The great cat had been stalking him even as he had been stalking The Bearded Ones. Suddenly it became very clear why Sabe had bellowed and charged into the bushes behind him. Sabe had saved his life! And in return Talks With The Animals had screamed at Sabe and chased him away.

Talks With The Animals felt sick, he had very nearly died. He was alive only because Sabe had seen The Long Toothed One and chased him away just in time. He had made another mistake that very nearly cost him his life. Actually he had made two mistakes. The first one was in not paying attention to what was going on around him, and the second one had been not believing in Sabe. They were two mistakes that he would never make again. He had surely been lucky this time, but next time he might not be.

He took off after Sabe but did not catch up until Sabe stopped beside the river. "I am sorry, Sabe, I will never doubt your loyalty again." He began scratching Sabe behind the ears again and did not stop until hours later.

"Well, we have had enough excitement for one day," he said. "I think we will rest here for the night."

The next morning the Bearded Ones were back at the river. Talks With The Animals decided to try his luck again. First he carefully scanned the area to be sure The Long Toothed One was not around. He slowly crept up to almost the same spot he was at yesterday and settled down to wait. This time he looked around frequently to be sure the Long Toothed One was not stalking him again. But the Long Toothed One was off stalking other prey.

Talks With The Animals waited patiently for the herd to finish watering and wander away to browse. Finally the herd started moving away from the river. But today they were taking a course that would take them too far away from his hiding place. He spotted the old bull with the limp and waited. The herd would pass him by too far away to use his spear. Maybe he could chase down the old bull anyway. The bull seemed to be even worse off today than before.

He waited until the herd was at its nearest point then he leaped to his feet and charged. Luckily the old bull was on the side of the herd nearest to him. At once the herd took off in a mad dash for the river. The old bull could still move surprisingly fast, but slowly he was left behind the herd. Talks With The Animals caught up with the bull and plunged the spear with all his might into it's ribcage just behind the bulls front leg. It angered the bull, which charged after Talks With The Animals. Talks With The Animals jumped out of the way just in time to keep from being gored by The Bearded One's horns.

Just then Sabe came crashing out of the jungle again. He charged after the old bull and ran into it headlong. The old bull was knocked off his feet. It would never rise again. It lay there and kicked it's feet for a few minutes before it finally bled to death. Talks With The animals squatted down to catch his breath. The Excitement of the hunt caused his heart to beat faster than the actual chase did. Sabe came up and stood over him as if he were standing guard. "Thanks Sabe, once again you saved the day for me," he said. "I will never doubt you again old friend. Between the two of us we make a great team."

Talks With The Animals finally got up and went to work on the old bull. Its meat would not be so tender as the young calf's would have been. But he was not complaining, here was enough meat to last for weeks. He would stay here in the little valley and smoke the meat. The horns of the bull could be made into tools. He had a lot of work to do.

Talks With The Animals set about cleaning the old bull immediately. First he stripped the hide from the carcass then he started cutting the meat into strips to be smoked. Suddenly he stopped what he was doing and stood up. He had no fire; how was he going to smoke the meat. He did not relish the thought of eating raw meat even though he had done it in the past. For the first few days the meat would not be too bad.

But after that it would start to rot. He would have to kill a large animal like The Bearded Ones or The White Tailed ones every few days to stay alive.

How did he keep getting himself into these fixes. He could bury the meat to make it last a few days longer. But if he did that he would be tied to that spot until the food ran out. The whole idea of this trip was to explore new territory. He could not do that if he had to stay near the herds of the bearded ones all of the time. He was going to have to think of something different. He cut out the animal's heart and moved to the shade of a small tree to eat it and think of a way to make a fire. The heart was one part of the animal that was always eaten raw.

He sat down in the shade and reached out one hand to hold himself up. It sure was getting hot today. It was mid day now and the rock beneath his hand was nearly hot enough to burn his hand. Suddenly he had an idea. Maybe he could lay the meat out to dry on the rocks. It just might work! He could cut the meat into narrow strips and lay it flat on the rocks. If he could keep the flying meat eaters away he might be able to dry the meat after all.

He quickly finished eating and set to work cutting up the meat into narrow strips. Then he began laying the meat out on the rocks in direct sunshine. He worked so fast that he began to sweat profusely. However he kept up the pace until his hands ached. Finally he sat down in the shade to rest. He still had several large pieces of meat left over.

He decided to put them in the water at the rivers edge to keep them cool. He could cut the rest of it up tomorrow. He was exhausted. He called out to Sabe who had been feeding near by.

Sabe came up to him and trumpeted as if asking, "What do you want?" He scratched him for a few minutes as always.

"Sabe, I need you to help me stand guard tonight. We must protect the meat until it has had a chance to dry out."

Sabe trumpeted softly again as if he understood. Talks With The Animals laid down to rest. With Sabe nearby he had nothing to worry about. He could trust Sabe's keen sense of hearing and smell to warn him of any danger.

Talks With The Animals awoke with a start. He was not sure why, maybe he had heard something that didn't sound quite right. When you spent most of your life in the wild you learned to ignore normal night sounds and at the same time pick out sounds that might bring danger. If you heard The Masked One rummaging around at night you didn't pay it any mind. But if you heard a herd of The Longnosed Ones moving around you had better be prepared to move quickly or you might get trampled.

He looked over to where Sabe was standing. Sabe was looking at the trees at the edge of the river intently. He seemed to be very agitated, he stood perfectly still. There must be something in the trees causing Sabe to act this way. Suddenly Sabe bellowed loudly and charged toward the trees. At the same time Talks With The Animals saw a shadow come charging out of the trees toward Sabe.

It was the Long Toothed One. Sabe came to a halt and trumpeted loudly, but The Long Toothed One didn't stop. It ran right up to Sabe and leaped onto his back. It began biting him on the neck. Sabe's skin was very tough and The Long Toothed One could not get a good bite. However the great teeth inflicted enough pain to make Sabe panic. He began twisting around franticly trying to get The Long Toothed One off his back.

Talks With The Animals had never seen The Long Toothed One attack a Long Nosed One before. But the great cat was driven mad by hunger. It was getting older and was not as fast and strong as it used to be. Most of the animals that it preyed on were no longer living. Once the great valley and the surrounding hills had supported dozens of The Long Toothed Cats. Now this was the only one left. The Long Toothed Ones were in direct competition with Talks With The Animal's clan for food. The Long Toothed Ones were solitary animals and did not normally show themselves around people.

Talks With The Animals grabbed up a spear and ran to Sabe's aid. Sabe had saved his life many times; and now it was his turn to defend Sabe. He shouted for Sabe to stand still, but it was useless. Sabe was bouncing around like something gone mad but he could not dislodge The Long Toothed One from his back. Talks With The Animals had to wait until he had a clear shot at the cat. Finally Sabe slowed down some and Talks With The Animals jumped forward and plunged his spear into the great cat's side. The cat let loose of Sabe and fell to the ground. But it was not dead yet! It turned and charged after Talks With The Animals. Talks With The Animals did not have time to run. He pulled his knife and crouched for the attack. The great cat leaped at him and they fell to the ground with the cat on top.

Talks With The Animals Plunged his knife into the great cat but still it did not die. The great cat opened his mouth and went for Talks With The Animals throat. Talks With The threw up his arms to fend off the attack. The great cat sunk teeth into his arm and began to shake his head. However the great cat was quickly getting weaker.

Even as the great cat bit down on Talks With The Animals arm Sabe charged in to help his master. Seeing his master in trouble had made Sabe forget his fears. He forgot about everynthing but saving his master. He grabbed the cat with his trunk and heaved mightily. The cat was lifted and thrown through the air. When Sabe picked him up his teeth pulled out of Talks With The Animals arm ripping out a chunk of flesh in the process.

The great cat landed hard and lay still as the life slowly drained out of him. He was the last of his kind. And another species of life on earth was gone for all time.

Luckily The Long Toothed One's teeth missed the bone. If his bone had been crushed he probably would have died here.

Talks With The Animals went down to the river and dug a handful of mud with his good arm. He packed the mud into the cuts to stop the bleeding and keep the wound from getting infected. He had seen a warrior that was gored in the leg one time survive the attack. But a moon later his leg had started to rot and he finally died from it. He really was not sure if the mud would keep his arm from doing the same thing. He could only wait and see.

After resting for a few minutes he got up and returned to where Sabe was standing. Sabe was bleeding from the neck but he was not seriously hurt. His thick hide had saved him from The Long Toothed One's huge teeth. He would be good as new in a couple of days. Talks With The Animals would not be so lucky. After seeing that Sabe was alright Talks With The Animals laid down to sleep.

He awoke late the next morning with a fever. He was too weak to cut any more meat into strips. He crawled over to where the strips of meat were and gathered some to eat. It was already getting hot again. He took as much of the meat as he could hold in one arm and struggled to his feet. He was very weak but he needed to find shelter from the sun. He slowly made his way back to the river's edge. He remembered there was a small waterfall close to where he had stashed the meat the day before.

Near the waterfall there was a small rock overhang that would provide shelter from the sun and rain. He stumbled into the shelter and collapsed. He lay for hours before being awakened by the late sun's rays coming into the shelter from a low angle. He felt even worse than before. He needed water badly.

He was too weak to stand so he crawled the few feet to the water's edge. He had to rest again for a few minutes before he was able to drink any water. Finally he drank all he could hold then crawled back to the shelter. He ate a couple pieces of the dried meat that he had brought then went back to sleep.

The next few days were a blur. He lost all sense of time as he struggled to stay alive. Finally on the third morning after crawling into the shelter, he came to his senses. He awoke with a thirst like he had never known before. He was still to weak to walk so once more he crawled to the river's edge to drink his fill. The water was cool and refreshing. He dunked his head under water for a few seconds to help clear his fuzzy brain. The water gave him strength. After resting for a few minutes he struggled to his feet and slowly walked back to the shelter.

He was going to live. His fate had been uncertain for a while but he was sure that he would make it now. He sat down and ate some of the meat strips. It didn't taste as good as smoked meat did but it was not bad, and it would keep him alive. He spent two more days at the shelter regaining his strength. He could feel his strength returning. He had always lived an active life and it served him well now. Finally he felt good enough to go out and find Sabe. He headed back to where the attack had occurred. There was Sabe contently eating away. And there on the rocks was all of the meat that he had cut into strips to dry. Sabe had stood guard over it the whole time he was sick. There was almost no vegetation left in a large circle around the whole area. Sabe had eaten every thing in sight, but he had not wandered off. Talks With The Animals went up to Sabe and gave him a great big hug.

Talks With The Animals spent the next week drying meat and making tools. He found some of the white rocks near the river and used the horns of The White Tail Ones to strike them until he had made enough points for two dozen spears. After the close call with The Long Toothed One he would always be sure to have more than one spear near to hand. His points were not as smooth and sharp as what someone like Square Jaw could make but they were getting better. He had discarded no more than half of the points that he started making. He could remember the time when he would make a dozen attempts at making a point before he had one that would work satisfactorily.

After making the points, Talks With The Animals went down to the river to select sticks to make the spears out of. He had to find just the right kind of wood. It had to be both straight and long. At the same time it had to be just the right diameter to fit his hands properly. His father had taught him to choose his spear shafts carefully for his life would one day depend on how well he made his weapons. Talks With The Animals had already found this to be true.

It took Talks With The Animals several hours to find enough shafts to make spears with. By the time he returned to camp it was getting dark again. He sat down and rested for a while, then he lay on his robes and slept. His arm was getting better every day but it still was sore and he had to rest frequently.

The next day was spent making spears. First he cut strips of rawhide from the skin of The Bearded One he had recently killed. Then he would select a point and a shaft. He had to split the shaft just right to make the point fit it.

After inserting the point into the shaft he would take the rawhide and wrap it around the shaft and point, stopping on each round to pull the rawhide tightly. After wrapping the shafts with rawhide he dipped them in the water to draw the rawhide tighter. After leaving the spears in the sun to dry for a while he smeared grease from The Bearded One on the rawhide to help preserve and hold it in place. He ended up discarding several points and shafts before he was through.

When he finished he had a half dozen spears ready for use, with another dozen points left over to make new spears as needed. He did not intend to be caught without tools again.

Talks With The Animals awoke to a warm morning. In addition to the dried meat from The Bearded One he was finding berries and other plants to eat also. He was ready. It was time to move on again. He set out following the river upstream again. After following the river for a day and a half he realized it was going higher and higher into the great hills. Finally he came to a place where the great hills rose almost straight up out of the river. The river got very narrow here and the water rushed through with tremendous speed and noise. They could go no further. He might be able to find a way through himself, but there was no hope for Sabe. The Long Nosed One was sure footed, but it was no way it could get through here. They would have to turn back.

Talks With The Animals camped there by the river and headed back the next day. When he got back to where the river made the turn toward the west, he camped at the same overhang near the river where he had stayed for days after being attacked by The Long Toothed One. Bright and early the next morning he set out once again. While going by the clearing where he had been attacked he saw the bones of The Long Toothed One. They had already been picked clean by hungry predators. He stopped to inspect the carcass more closely. One of the teeth from its skull had come loose and was lying nearby. He decided to keep it. He added it to the small leather bag that he kept with him at all times.

His father had started a tradition when he kept a claw and some teeth from the bear that he had fought and killed. Now all of the warriors had leather pouches slung around their necks with certain items inside that were important to them.

"Well Sabe, let's be moving on, I want to see some new country," He said to Sabe as he headed south again. He spent most of the day exploring the little valley as he slowly made his way south. All day long the great hill to his left seemed to be getting lower and lower. Finally when he had traveled almost the whole length of the valley the hill suddenly ended abruptly. It was a good thing that it did end for at the southern end of the valley lay another great hill. When he finally reached the very end of the valley he could see a pass between the great hill to his left and the great hill that was at the southern end of the valley. "Well Sabe, we will camp here tonight and start anew in the morning," he said. Right where the valley ended there were two small streams that joined to form a larger one.

Suddenly Talks With The Animals realized that the water was flowing the opposite way from the river he had followed into this valley. When he was following the river before he had been going upstream. Even though he was still going south he was now going downstream. If the river he followed out of the great valley could lead him into these great hills then maybe he could follow these streams downstream to get back out of these great hills! He decided immediately that is just what he was going to do.

The next day he set off to follow the stream downstream. Every now and then the stream was joined by another one. Each time the stream got a little bigger. Late that afternoon the stream he was following was joined by another stream that was even bigger. Where they joined the stream became as large as the river he had followed before. He was sure that his idea was going to work now. All he had to do was keep following the stream downstream and sooner or later he would find flat country again. But he could see another great hill in front of him. Would he really be able to get through?

Talks With The Animals made camp and settled down for the night. As always, Sabe was grazing nearby. Talks With The Animals thought of his clan again. He wondered how everyone was doing. He missed his parents but at the same time he was really enjoying this time away from the clan.

His thoughts turned once again to Deer Pawn and his heart became heavy. He had no right to think of her. She was with Swims Like A Fish. He hoped they were happy together. Maybe he should have told her how he felt. But it was too late now, he could never tell her how he felt if she wanted Swims Like A Fish.

Well he did not have to go back home. He could always stay out here own his own. Just him and Sabe. At least this way he was free. He could go where he pleased and do what he pleased. He did not have to worry about finding food for anyone but himself. But he knew that he would go back to his clan someday.

Suddenly he heard one of the singing dogs. It was a lonesome mourning sound. That was a sound he had not heard for quite some time. Not only that, there seemed to be different kinds of animals in this area. He had not seen The Stinking One since leaving the great valley. That was okay with him though. If you saw The Stinking One raise his tail you had better be moving on. The Stinking One was a small furry animal but it's smell was awful.

Come to think of it he had not seen any Longnosed Ones since leaving the great valley either. What Talks With The Animals did not know is The Longnosed Ones were almost gone. They had once roamed all of North America, but now the last herds were confined to the great valley.

His thoughts were interrupted by The Singing Dog again. Somehow it did not sound right. It was like it was in pain or suffering in some way. Talks With The Animals decided to turn in for the night. He lay down and was soon asleep.

He was awakened several times during the night by The Singing Dog. Finally by dawn the next morning he could take no more. The singing dog's voice sounded weaker every time he heard it. He decided to go and investigate.

He waited until he heard it again to pinpoint the direction the sound was coming from. Then he set off to see what was going on. Twenty minutes later he finally found the singing dog. It was laying on its side whimpering. But when it saw Talks With The Animals it began to growl weakly.

Talks With The Animals could see blood around its mouth and on its paws. It was obvious that the animal had been hurt and was in pain.

Talks With The Animals began to talk slowly to the animal hoping to calm it down some. He slowly moved forward as he was talking. Finally he was only five feet away from the dog. He could see some strange little sticks poking out from the dogs face and forepaws. These were what was causing all the pain. The dog growled as he took the last few feet to its side. But it was too tired and weak to put up any resistance. Talks With The Animals slowly pulled the little sticks out of the dogs face. He wondered what or who had done this to the poor dog. He took one of the little sticks and looked it over carefully. He carelessly rubbed his thumb over the end of it. That was a mistake, it pricked him painfully and a small bead of blood appeared on the end of his thumb.

Talks With The Animals heard something scratching around in the underbrush. Remembering The Long Toothed One he decided to go and see what it was. He grabbed up a spear in each hand and cautiously approached the bushes where the sound was coming from. He used the spear in his left hand to part the bushes while he held a spear at the ready in his right hand. When he parted the bushes a small animal made a kind of hissing noise at him and started backing away.

The animal was covered from head to toe with the little sticks, yet it did not seem to be in any pain. The animal turned around and ambled away. As it did so it brushed up against the trunk of a small tree, and several of the small sticks stuck into it. However, the little animal walked away as if nothing was wrong. Talks With The Animals went over to look at the little sticks in the tree. This time he did not touch them. They were the same thing that he had pulled out of the singing dog. So that's where the little sticks came from. He remembered Square Jaw telling of just such an animal with very sharp sticks growing out of it. At the time no one had believed Square Jaw. But now he had seen it with his own eyes. What a strange creature! Talks With The animals wondered what other magical creatures were out there that he had never seen.

He heard the singing dog whimper again and returned to his side. This time the dog didn't even lift its head. Talks with the animals was not sure that it would live. He scooped it up in his arms and returned to camp. He laid it gently on his skins and went to get water for it. When he returned he dribbled a little in the dog's mouth. This seemed to revive it somewhat. It struggled briefly then settled back down. It lay there looking at Talks With The Animals. However it did not growl anymore. It was as if the dog understood that Talks With The Animals was trying to help it.

Talks With The Animals decided to try and nurse the dog back to health. But if he was going to do this he would need meat. He only had a few days' supply of the dried meat left.

He stayed with the dog all night talking soothingly and giving it some water occasionally. The next morning the dog appeared to be resting fairly well so he decided to leave it long enough to find food. He called out to Sabe to stay close to camp while he was gone. Somehow Sabe understood that he should guard the dog.

Talks With The Animals walked downstream looking for something to kill for food. He had only been looking for twenty minutes or so when he came across a small herd of the White Tailed Ones. They were feeding quietly near the river. He slowly circled to his left to make sure he was downwind of them. Then he began to slowly creep up on the herd. It took him a half hour to get within spear range.

Finally he picked his target and slung his spear with careful aim. It caught the White Tailed in the neck and it turned to run away. It bleated loudly and the whole herd turned and bounded away. However the spear got caught in some low bushes and tripped the White Tailed One that Talks With The Animals had speared. It went down hard and struggled to get back up. Talks With The Animals quickly ran forward and thrust another spear into the animal's side to end its suffering. Talks With The Animals did not have any qualms about killing for food, but at the same time he did not want the animal to suffer any longer than necessary.

He shouldered the animal and started back to his camp. He would have plenty of meat for a while. He could feed the dog some and cut up strips to dry in the sun again. It certainly was hot enough now to dry the meat out. The cold season would be here before long, but it was still hot enough now to cause Talks With The Animals to sweat profusely. He had to stop and rest twice before he made it back to camp.

Finally he struggled back to camp and dropped wearily to the ground. After resting for a few minutes he went over and checked on the dog. It lifted its head weakly and whimpered at him. Talks With The Animals put his hand out slowly to rub his head. After a few minutes he went and got his water skin and filled it with fresh water from the river.

Then he returned to camp and cut off meat for the dog. But it was so weak that it could not eat it. Talks With The Animals had to cut the meat into small chunks that the dog could swallow without chewing. The dog managed to swallow a few small pieces and drink a little water; then it lay back, exhausted.

Talks With The Animals started cleaning the White Tailed One and cut the meat into long slender strips to dry in the sun. He worked until sundown. Even after the sun went down it was still hot so he went and took a swim in the river.

The next morning the dog managed to sit up and eat a fairly good meal. Talks With The Animals was sure that he would live now. He spent two weeks nursing the dog back to health. At first, Sabe would not come anywhere near the dog.

But as the days slowly passed by Sabe began to accept the Dog's presence. By the time two weeks had passed Sabe and the dog were friends. One morning Talks With The Animals got up and decided it was time to be moving on again.

Chapter 9: The River

The water looked inviting, and Talks With The Animals was very hot. He had been traveling all day long. He had to backtrack several times to find a way through that Sabe could follow. Since leaving his last camp where he had nursed The Singing Dog back to health the progress had been very slow.

Each day the land became a little flatter and the stream that he was following got a little bigger. His idea had worked; he had found another way out of the Great Hills.

Finally he could take no more. He quickly unloaded his and Sabe's pack and jumped into the river. The water was quite deep and slow moving here. He was instantly cooled by the water. He dove under and swam for a ways under water. When he came up The Singing Dog was running franticly back and forth along the river bank and yelping furiously.

When it saw Talks With The Animals surface it jumped into the water and swam out to where Talks With The Animals was.

"What's the matter? Were you afraid I had drowned? he laughingly asked the dog as it swam up to him. He reached out and patted the dog's head. Then he headed back to shore with the dog close behind him. Sabe was standing in the water near shore. He drew large amounts of water into his long nose and sprayed it all over himself. When Talks The Animals got close enough to the shore where he could stand up he started splashing water at Sabe. Sabe filled his long nose with water and sprayed Talks With The Animals with great relish. They splashed around the water for a while, then Talks With The Animals crawled out to lie in the sun and dry off. Sabe began feeding contentedly nearby and The Singing Dog came and laid down next to Talks With The Animals.

Talks With The Animals reached out and patted The Singing Dog playfully. Talks With The Animals was content. For the first time since leaving the clan he was happy. He still thought of Deer Pawn, but it did not make him feel so sad anymore. Somehow he had a feeling that she missed him and would wait for him to return. He was not sure how he knew this but he was sure it was true.

"Hey, this is the life isn't it? he spoke to The Singing Dog. "We get up when we want, we go where we want, and do what we want." Talks With The Animals took a nap. When he woke up a half hour later he was hot again. But the sun was finally starting to set and it was a little cooler. He sat up and reached over to pet The Singing Dog. "I am going to have to come up with a name for you," he said to the dog. Since the dog had gotten well he had not left Talks With The Animal's side. "Let's see, what would be a good name for you. How about Hannock?" he asked the dog, as if it could understand. The Singing Dog just looked at him and barked.

"No, that's no good, let's try something else. I know, how about Oshkosh. That's it; your name will be Oshkosh. The singing dog just jumped around and bit at Talks With The Animals playfully.

"Yes, Oshkosh is the perfect name for you. Since it means to always be happy. That sure describes you doesn't it? You always seem to be in a good mood. Next to Sabe you are my best friend.

And so it went for the next couple of weeks. The three companions slowly made their way downstream. They stopped to hunt occasionally and slept whenever they wanted.

The stream kept getting bigger and bigger. Almost every day they had to cross a stream that flowed into the great river.

One day Talks With The Animals came to a cliff near the river. It was as high as the trees, and was almost a straight drop to the river below. Here the river picked up speed and roared over the rocks with gusto. The water was churned up into a white froth. Talks With The Animals was surprised. He had not seen white water like this since he left the great hills behind. There were great boulders strewn around haphazardly as if some great spirit had tossed them at random into the river.

From his view point Talks With The Animals could see a long section of the river. There were small clearings on both sides of the river. Looking down stream he could see the slope gradually going down to meet the river perhaps a twenty minute walk away. He could see that there were many more trees here than it was in The Great Valley. He wondered if there were any of The Longnosed ones here. He had not seen a Longnosed One since leaving The Great Valley.

He could see several of The White Tailed Ones feeding in the small valley. There was the sound of The Flying Ones all around him. Just then movement caught his eye. There on the other side of The Great River he could see a small herd of The Bearded Ones.

Then he heard a loud noise that made him jump. It came from the trees above his head. Rat a tat tat, there it goes again. Talks With The Animals looked all around him. Finally he saw one of The Flying Ones. It was large and had a red head that came to a sharp point. Below the read head he could see a couple black and white stripes on its neck. The rest of its body was black with just a little white on its wings.

Just as he spotted it, he saw it beat its head against the tree trunk. Again the sound came, rat a tat tat. Talks With The Animals had never seen anything like it before.

What sort of animal would beat its head against a tree with such force? Talks With The Animals decided that he would not go any further until he had explored this area.

Talks With The Animals put up his shelter made from the hides of The Bearded Ones. Usually he just slept on the ground but he was going to stay here for a while. He had explored the cliff looking for a cave or a place the cliff might lean out enough to protect him from the weather, but he could not find a suitable spot. Finally he decided to put his shelter next to the trunk of a great tree growing about halfway up the hill that led to the cliff.

His food supplies were running low again, and he would have to go hunting soon. But for today he was just going to set up camp and then rest for a while. After getting his shelter set up he opened his packs and looked over his belongings. He was down to two spears, but he had enough points left to make several more. There was enough food to last maybe two or three more days. Tomorrow he would cut a few small trees and make several more spears. Then he would go on the hunt.

Talks With The Animals was up early the next morning. He

wanted to cut the shafts he needed to make spears. He set out to find the right kind of small trees to cut. He quickly found what he was looking for and set to work cutting them down. It was hot strenuous work. Finally he had enough cut, and stripped of limbs to make a half dozen spears with. He decided to sit down and rest some before returning to camp with his shafts. He selected a large tree and sat down with his back against it. He closed his eyes and drifted off to sleep. He could trust his ever-present companion, Oshkosh, to alert him to any danger. Though it had only been about one moon since he had discovered The Singing Dog and come to its aid, he trusted it completely.

Suddenly he heard Oshkosh growling quietly. He opened his eyes and spoke quietly to Oshkosh to calm him down. He heard something scratching around in the undergrowth only a short distance away. Oshkosh was standing and looking intently in the direction the sounds were coming from. He did not appear to be afraid, it was more like he sensed food. Talks With The Animals reached out to pet Oshkosh and spoke quietly to him again. He commanded Oshkosh to sit and he obediently did so.

Talks With The Animals picked up his spears and slowly crept toward the bushes where the scratching sound was coming from. Then he heard another strange noise; gobble gobble gobble. It was The Great Walking Birds that he had heard scratching. Talks With The Animal's mouth began to water as he thought of the prospect of eating one of The Great Walking Birds. He knelt down and leaned forward very cautiously. These birds were always alert and very hard to capture. Most of the time you only glimpsed one when it took flight because something had disturbed it. They were very had to sneak up on.

But Talks With The Animals was going to try his luck. He had not tasted one of the birds in many moons and they were good eating. He moved ever so slowly toward the area where they were scratching and feeding. He would only get one chance. Once the birds detected him, they would be gone in a flash.

Finally he came up to the bushes where the birds were feeding. He watched for a few minutes to see how many birds there were. He could see four birds busily scratching and feeding, and one of them was only ten feet away. He braced himself and made ready to attack. His aim must be true, for there would not be a second chance.

He waited until the one closest to him had his head down and was facing away from him. Suddenly he lunged forward and threw his spear. It struck The Great Bird with such force that it was thrown several feet away. However, it was not dead yet. The spear had only grazed it along its back and punctured the wing on the other side of its body. The bird quickly got its feet squawking loudly and tried to fly away.

Talks With The Animals did a nose dive for the great bird just as the rest of the little flock took flight in a great rush of air and squawking. He managed to grab one wing only to have the bird turn on him and start pecking furiously. He let go and covered his head to protect himself from the frenzied bird. The spear broke loose and The Great Bird tried to fly away again, but its wing was broken and it could no longer fly.

Talks With The Animals picked up his spear and chased after The Great Bird all the while calling to Oshkosh for help. He made a mad dash for The Great Bird but it swerved away at the last moment. Talks With The Animals tried to turn after the fleeing bird but only managed to run headlong into a tree. He hit the tree so hard that he was knocked flat on his back. He hollowed out loud, "Ouch, where did that stupid tree come from?"

Suddenly he saw Oshkosh go streaking by, chasing after the bird. After several attempts it managed to catch the wounded bird by the neck and bring it down. Talks With The Animals sat up slowly. He had a headache coming on big time.

He swore to himself, "That's the last time I try to chase down one of The Great Walking Birds." Oshkosh returned to Talks With The Animals with The Great Walking Bird in its mouth and placed it at his feet. Then Oshkosh sat down and looked up at Talks With The Animals and started howling.

Somehow, Talks With The Animals got the feeling that Oshkosh was making fun of him. Talks With The Animals just glared at Oshkosh and stooped to pick up The Great Walking Bird. He had to straighten up slowly because he was still dizzy from hitting the tree.

Talks With The Animals stood still a few minutes to let the cobwebs clear from his brain. Finally he called to Oshkosh and headed for camp. Just as he returned to camp he remembered that he had gone out today to get shafts to make more spears with. But he had forgotten all about them when he saw the turkeys. He hollowed out loud, "Oh great, I forgot the shafts for the spears. Well they can wait until tomorrow, my head hurts to much now."

Talks With The Animals woke up the next morning with a headache. He had a nice knot on his forehead where he ran into the tree. When he stood up he became dizzy and had to stand still until it passed. After waiting a few minutes he set off to find the shafts he had cut for his spears. Presently he found them and returned to camp. He spent the rest of the day making new spears.

He took it easy for a few days while his head healed. Finally he decided to go hunting for one of The Bearded Ones. He called to Sabe and Oshkosh to follow along. After looking for several hours the only Bearded Ones he had seen were on the move. He could not get close enough to get a good shot with his spear. He could see a herd across the river from him that seemed to be much more calm than the small herd on this side of the river. He decided that he would have to cross the river.

He noticed that the river spread out and became very wide and shallow downstream from the cliffs. Maybe he could find a way across there. He headed downstream until he came to a place where it looked shallow enough to cross. It was getting later in the warm season now and the water had already dropped several feet since he arrived. He stepped gingerly out into the water. It was cool and refreshing, but he still had to be careful. He didn't want to fall in here.

The water only came to his waist, but if he fell he would be swept downstream. Carefully he took one step after another with Sabe following along behind him. Oshkosh had not worked up enough nerve to follow along yet. He was running back forth along the river bank and yelping excitedly. Talks With The Animals ignored him for now. He would be alright while Talks With The Animals hunted for The Bearded Ones.

Talks With The Animals was almost halfway across the river when something hit his leg. He looked down just in time to see a silver flash through the water. It was a great fish.

Here was food that he had not even thought of lately. He had not eaten fish since leaving The Great Valley. He stepped over to lean against a huge boulder laying in mid stream to rest for a minute. When he looked down he could see several of the fish swimming around in a circle on the downstream side of the rock. He threw his spear at one without even thinking. As luck would have it the fish was impaled on the end of his spear. The fish began writhing around frantically trying to get away. Talks With The Animals almost lost his grip on the spear. He managed to hang on and get his balance.

He quickly pulled the spear up out of the water. There on the end of it was a fish as long as his arm with stripes down its side. He had never seen a fish like this before. He decided to try his luck again instead of going after The Bearded Ones. If he could not catch anymore then he could always continue his hunt for The Bearded Ones.

He pulled the fish off the spear and laid it in a depression on top of the boulder. Then he took up his spear and started looking for more fish in the water. Suddenly he saw another and hurriedly jabbed his spear at it. This time he missed. He kept jabbing his spear every time he saw one of the silver flashes. After several more tries he managed to spear another one. Since Sabe was standing nearby spraying himself with the cool water he called him over. He took one of his skin pouches that he used for storage from Sabe's back pack and put both fish in it.

He fished for another hour and managed to spear ten more of the fish. Then on his next try he missed the fish and slipped. He let go of the spear and grabbed for the boulder to keep from losing his balance. When he did so his spear fell into the water and was immediately washed away. Well he had more spears, so it wasn't a great loss. He decided he had enough for one day and headed back to shore. Upon reaching shore he took one of the fish from his pouch and tossed it to Oshkosh. He returned to camp with the remaining fish and set to work cleaning them.

They really were big fish. After cleaning them he cut them

up in strips to dry in the sun. He grabbed a few pieces from the first one he cut up and began eating them as he cut the others up. "Oh my, that is some good eating," he said out loud. "I believe I could spend the rest of my life here along this river. There is so much good food I do not know what to eat next." He wondered what he would run into next here in this wonderful little valley by the river.

He laid the fish out on the rocks in the sun to dry. Some of the meat from The Great Walking Bird was already dry so he put it in a pouch for storage. Life was good. He had so many different kinds of food here he didn't need The Bearded Ones for food. He ate one final piece of the fish he had speared and lay down to nap.

Those fish were so good he must think of a name for them. Thinking of the stripes going down there sides, he decided to call them The Striped Ones. As usual with his people, he gave them a name that also described them.

Talks With The Animals went back to the river over the next several days and caught many more fish to dry in the sun. He could tell that the days were getting shorter now, and the fish were taking much longer to dry.

One day he surprised a White Tailed One and managed to spear it before it could get away. He also cut this up to dry in the sun.

With the days getting shorter he would need to put up a supply of food to get him through the winter. He did not worry too much about Sabe, and Oshkosh. They were both wild animals and could find enough food to last the winter.

A few days later he awoke to a cool morning; the cold season would be here soon. He decided to try again for one of The Bearded Ones. He called Sabe and took off across the river.

He could see a small herd of The Bearded Ones grazing near the top of the cliff. If he and Sabe could get in behind them he might be able to corner one. If he still had fire he could have driven them right off the cliff without any problem. But then again, if he had wings he could fly at them and chase them off the cliff too. It was no use wishing for something he did not have. He would have to make do with what he had.

The cliff on this side of the river was not quite as high or steep, but it was still plenty high enough to kill The Bearded Ones if he could somehow drive them over the cliff. Luckily they were approaching downwind from the herd.

He reached up and gently scratched Sabe to keep him quite while he came up with a plan. He finally decided the direct approach was the best. He and Sabe would simply burst out of the woods and charge straight after the herd. With luck he would be able to spear one during the confusion that would follow before the herd could get together and stampede away.

"Okay Sabe, are you ready?" he whispered. He was sure that Sabe understood what he wanted to do. Suddenly he slapped Sabe on the tail and let out with a war whoop as he charged into the clearing. Sabe bellowed loudly as they broke out of the clearing. Caught unaware, the small herd broke into a mass confusion of milling bodies bouncing and running in every direction.

Talks With The Animals could see a bull and several steers running parallel with the cliff. He quickly turned to head them off. The lead bull caught sight of Talks With The Animals and charged at him. However Sabe saw the bull and ran ahead to meet it headlong. They ran into each other at full speed. One of the bulls horns penetrated Sabe's thick hide and the shock of it knocked the bull off its feet. Talks With The Animals quickly ran forward and jabbed a spear into the bull before it could get up.

It was over almost as quickly as it had started. The bull lay on its side and slowly bled to death. Talks With The Animals went to Sabe's side to check on him. The bull horn had broken off from the force and still protruded from Sabe's shoulder. He scratched Sabe and talked softly as he looked at the wound. There was only one thing to do; he was going to have to pull the horn out. He grabbed it and jerked mightily. The horn popped out and he went flying backwards. Sabe gave a loud bellow when the horn pulled out, but he stood his ground and did not move.

Talks With The Animals got to his feet and returned to look at the wound. It was not as bad as he first thought. It was about half the size of the palm of his hand and maybe half that deep. Talks With The Animals led Sabe down the hill to the river's edge. He scooped up water and washed out the wound then he grabbed a double handful of mud and pressed it into the wound.

"Well Sabe old buddy, it's not much; but it's all that I know how to do," he said. Sabe just shook his head as if it was nothing and headed back up the hill. There was work to be done. He knew his master would load him up with meat from The Bearded One to take back across the river. Talks With The Animals followed Sabe back up the hill and set to work on the carcass.

He decided to cut the meat up and let it dry on this side of the river so Sabe could get plenty of rest. Three days later Talks With The Animals loaded Sabe up with dried meat and they headed back across the river. Talks With The Animals now had all the food he needed to get through the coming cold season. He used the hide from The Bearded One to make a another warm set of clothes. He wanted to be prepared.

A few days later Talks With The Animals woke up to a light frost. The cold season was on the way. He spent the next few weeks collecting shafts and rocks so he could make plenty of tools during the long winter months. Finally one day it started to snow. The cold season was here, but he was ready. He had laid in a store of food for himself. He had even spent a few days collecting grass and storing it to help Sabe make it through the winter.

The snow quickly melted and it became warm for a few more days. Talks With The Animals used this time to explore the area around him. He walked down river for several hours one day until he came to a place where the water no longer rushed over the large boulders. Here the water made one last mad rush over the rocks before calming down. He noticed that there were still a few grapes hanging on the vines here.

He had been eating them ever since he made his permanent camp here on the river. They were very good. And there were so many of them he could hardly believe his eyes when he first encountered them along the river. There had been a few vines growing in the great valley where the clan was. He noticed that there seemed to be more and more of them the further down the river he came.

Finally when he decided to make his permanent camp at the cliff up the river, he could see large vines growing in the woods down river from the cliff. But nothing could prepare him for the sheer number of vines growing here. And the size of the vines was unbelievable; some of them were almost as big around as his waist. A few days before the cold weather came the vines were loaded with so many grapes it looked like some of the great trees were going to snap under the weight.

There were so many wonderful things here along the river that Talks With The Animals thought he was in the land of the Great Spirits. He never knew what new and exciting thing he would encounter next. When he returned to the clan he sure would have some great stories to tell. He was not sure anyone would believe him. If he had not seen these things with his own eyes he might not believe it himself.

He began picking up grapes and putting them in his pouch. They were starting to shrivel up but were still edible. He better enjoy these while he could because they would be gone soon. After that he would only have dried meat to make it through the long winter moons.

After filling his pouch he headed back to his camp for the day. He did not want to be caught away from shelter at night. It may be warm now but the nights could get cold very quickly when the sun went to sleep for the night. There had already been one snow, or White Rain as he liked to call it; and another would come soon he was sure.

Talks With The Animals was right. Just a few days later it began to snow again. But he was not worried, he had a sturdy shelter and plenty of warm robes thanks to The Bearded Ones and The White Tailed Ones. His people had learned long ago to use almost every part of an animal. The meat was used for food and the hide was used for clothes and moccasins.

The hide could also be cut into very narrow strips and used to tie things together with. Even the bones and antlers were used as tools.

He busied himself through the long winter days making tips

for his spears. He could see a marked improvement in his tips; they were much sharper and had better points than the ones he made during the warm season. He began to experiment with different designs. Some he made very broad and heavy for large animals while others were long and slender to spear The Striped Fish with. He had long ones, short ones, fat ones, skinny ones, and every other combination he could think of.

Once he was satisfied with these he set to the large bundle of sticks he had cut and began fashioning shafts to mount his many tips on. He also experimented with different shaft lengths and thickness. Once again he experimented with different tips on different shafts. He would try one point on a shaft and heft it and practice throwing it outside when the weather permitted. When he was done he had about twenty spears ready for use and twice that many extra points.

He had short slender shafts with thin pointed tips for throwing long distances and long heavy shafts for jabbing at large animals. He even took one shaft and cut two shorter pieces from it to make knives with. Finally he could do no more. He had all the weapons he could possibly use, even more than he really wanted to carry. He decided he had better find something else to do, since the cold season was not over yet.

One day after going out and checking on Sabe he came back to the shelter with cold, wet feet. He removed his moccasins and massaged his feet to get them warm again.

He took one of the extra hides he had and began cutting pieces to make moccasins. In the past his mother always made them, but she was not here now so he would have to do it.

He tried on the first pair he made but the left one was too short to fit over his foot and the right one was long enough but not wide enough. This business of making moccasins was not so easy. His respect for his mother grew with each pair he made that would not fit just right. Finally he had an idea. He would take the rawhide out of his old moccasins and lay them on the piece of hide. All he had to do was cut around the edges of the old one and he would have pieces of the new hide the same size.

He quickly took his old ones and set to work. A couple of hours later he had a pair of moccasins that fit quite well. They were not as good as what his mother made but they would keep his feet warm. He used up the remainder of the hide making more pairs. When he was finished he had three spare pairs and a whole pile of hide scraps.

Now if the cold season would leave and let the warm season return he could return home. Well at least with his new moccasins he could go out in the snow and not get his feet wet. He went out to check on Sabe at least once every day.

He was getting worried about Sabe. He was looking like he was not getting enough to eat. There were only a couple more armloads of the grass left that he had collected for Sabe.

He still had plenty of dried meat left for himself, and Oshkosh was able to find enough small game to feed himself.

One day he saw Sabe eating bark off of the trees nearby. Suddenly he remembered the pile of bark shavings left from the spears he had made. If Sabe could eat bark from a large tree then surely he could eat the bark from the small trees used to make spears with.

He went back to his shelter and grabbed a armful of the bark shavings and returned to Sabe. Sabe trumpeted happily when he saw Talks With Animals coming with a armload of food.

When Talks With The Animals laid the bark shavings on the ground Sabe began to eat with gusto. Talks With The Animals went back down to the river's edge where he had collected the shafts for his spears and began cutting all the saplings in sight. He carried a couple arm loads back to Sabe then returned to his shelter. He was dead tired. He would not be able to go on like this every day for a long period of time. But the air did not seem quite as cold lately; maybe the cold season would be leaving soon.

Talks With The Animals was right; the days were starting to get a little longer. Spring would be here soon. He managed to kill another one of The Great Walking Birds, much to his delight. It was a welcome change from the dried meat he had been eating all winter. He still had enough of the dried meat to last another moon. It was not as fresh as when he first made it but it would keep him alive. Soon he would be making the journey back home.

Chapter 10: Talks With The Animals returns Home

Talks With The Animals stood on the natural bridge and looked out over the valley. He was nearly home. If he really pushed hard then by this time tomorrow he should be back with the clan. He had spent the last two moons making his way back home. He could have gotten back faster but he had taken time to explore some of the small streams that joined with the river. Now he was back in The Great Valley. A whole year had passed since he last stood on this huge rock and gazed out over the valley.

Now he was excited and sad at the same time. Soon he would see his parents again and the little one. And then he would see Deer Pawn. Would she want to see him? At one time he was sure she was waiting for him and the very next minute he was not sure. Maybe Swims Like A Fish had already taken her as his mate. After all he had been gone for a whole year. A lot could happen in that time.

Only time would tell. He decided that he would accept what ever he found when he got back. He and Deer Pawn and Swims Like A Fish had grown up together. They had been through some hard times together and had always been friends. He would not change that now.

Suddenly he saw movement far to the north. But just as quick as he spotted it, it disappeared back into the forest. He strained his eyes trying to see what it was, but it was no Use. Whatever it was it was gone now. He decided to wait a while to see if he could catch sight of it again. Finally he saw movement again.

He was not sure but that looked like another person or maybe several people walking. But what would the clan be doing so far south. His heart was racing now at the prospect of seeing another person. It had been over a year since he left the clan. In all that time he had only Sabe and Oshkosh for companions. But no, he must be seeing things; no one from the clan was likely to be this far south. There it was again, he could see them more clearly now.

It was people! He climbed down from the huge rock bridge and hurried off to intercept the hunting party. It had to be a hunting party. That was the only thing that made sense. He was so excited that he began running in the direction that the party was going. A half an hour later he stopped to listen for the hunting party. If he was not careful he might miss them all together.

He climbed up on a small outcrop of rocks to look for the hunting party. Just as he reached the top he could hear voices. "I tell you that I saw somebody over this way," he heard one of the party say.

"Swims Like A Fish you are seeing things, there is no one around here but us," he heard someone reply.

He called out loudly, "I would not be so sure of that if I were you." The whole hunting party made a mad dash for the nearest cover upon hearing this. Talks With The Animals began laughing loudly at this. "What is the matter, Swims Like A Fish? Are you afraid of voices in the jungle?" he asked merrily.

At this Swims Like A Fish stood up and grinned from ear to ear. "I thought I recognized your voice, Talks With The Animals." At this, Talks With The Animals jumped down from the rocks and Swims Like A Fish hurried over to him and gave him a big bear hug.

"It is good to see you again, my friend. It has been a long time. The clan had given you up for dead. That is, everyone except Deer Pawn. She always insisted you would return one day. In fact she has kept me about half convinced that you would return. Now I see she was right."

Finally the other members of the hunting party came out and greeted Talks With The Animals. Talks With The Animals recognized Swims Like A Fish but there were several more warriors that he did not recognize. Swims Like A Fish saw him looking at the strangers and spoke up, "It is Okay, these are friends of ours.

"These people came over the Great Hill just like we did.

They arrived at our camp only a few days after you left. We almost fought with them but The Wise One commanded us to hold back. Instead of going to meet the new people with spears at the ready, he insisted that we arm ourselves with food instead. It was a wise decision, for we could see that their people were almost starving to death just as our clan was when we came into the valley. Their whole clan dropped their weapons as one and fell to eating voraciously.

Their clan numbered only fifteen people when they joined us. They were once many more people where they lived before but they had started running out of food. So finally one day their clan split up into two groups. Half of the group stayed behind while the other half set off to find a new home where there was more food. However, they did not have very good luck. Most of their clan died from starvation before reaching this valley. We invited them to settle here in The Great Valley with us. Our clan had fed well since coming here and we wanted to share our wealth with these newcomers.

"You won't believe your eyes when you return. There are many little ones now. Even I have taken a woman and have a little one born only a moon ago."

Talks With The Animals heart skipped a beat. So Swims Like A Fish and Deer Pawn had gotten together after all. Suddenly he did not feel so happy about returning to the clan. He looked at his old friend and congratulated him. "I hope you and Deer Pawn are happy," he managed to mumble.

Swims Like A Fish looked at him with amusement. He could not resist picking on Talks With The Animals. "Oh, its a great life. I have a wonderful woman who takes care of my every need and want while I am at home. And the little one is a joy to behold. I could not be happier. At this Talks With The Animals hung his head and started to turn away.

Swims Like A Fish decided he had gone far enough. "Wait, Talks With The Animals, I have not told you the best part yet." Talks With The Animals turned around, he really did not want to hear anymore about Swims Like A Fish and Deer Pawn.

But he had grown up with them, how could he not listen to what Swims Like A Fish had to say?

"I have the most beautiful woman in the clan. And to think, only a little over a year ago I did not even know that she existed." This did not make Talks With The Animals feel any better. He agreed with Swims Like A Fish. Deer Pawn was the most beautiful woman he had ever known.

Suddenly it dawned on him what Swims Like A Fish said. "What do you mean, you did not know she existed a year ago?" he asked. "You have known Deer Pawn for your whole life."

Swims Like A Fish took pity on Talks With The Animals. "Of course I have known Deer Pawn all of my life. But I did not take Deer Pawn for my mate. My woman came over The Great Hills with her clan. I did not meet her until after you were already gone last year."

Talks With The Animals heard him but he still could not believe it. "You mean you did not take Deer Pawn as your woman?" he asked.

"Of course not," Swims Like A Fish replied. "Everyone in the clan knew that she was going to be your mate. Except maybe you. Oh, I tried to win her over, but it was no use.

Every time I saw her, all she would talk about was you. About how brave and good you were. I could not even get a word in edgewise. I was a year older than you and at one time I thought that I would be a better warrior than you. But Deer Pawn always knew that you were the better of us. However she did not hold that against me. She said that you would be her choice regardless of how you turned out. There was nothing that I could do to change her mind. Finally I gave up even trying to win her over."

Talks With The Animals could not believe his ears. " But before I left the clan last year, every time I would go to see Deer Pawn she would be with you." he blurted out. "She was only trying to make you jealous." Swims Like A Fish replied. "She made me hang out with her. She was afraid that you did not want her and she was trying to make you jealous so you would want her. But it backfired. You ended taking off without even saying goodbye to her. She would not even speak to me for weeks after you left. Finally she came to me one day and told me to go and bring you back. She insisted that you left the clan because of her.

She even said that she would leave the clan if it would make you come back.

I tried to talk some sense into her, but she would not listen. Finally about a moon ago she said she would go and look for you herself if I would not go. I finally gave in and told her I would go.

Talks With The Animals felt much better now. Deer Pawn had waited for him all this time. When he got to the clan she would not have to wait anymore. He was going to tell her right away that he loved her. He would never leave her again without telling her he loved her first.

"To tell the truth I was kind of envious of you. You were brave enough to go off on the hunt by yourself. By now my woman was heavy with child and I was afraid to leave her side for more than a few hours at a time. But finally the little one came. I waited for almost a full moon to make sure that they would be Okay without me. "Deer Pawn was after me every day to go and find you.

She promised that she would spend every spare moment helping my mate with her child until I returned. So we set off a couple of days ago; not only to look for you but to explore the valley. Somehow The Wise One knew that you had traveled south. Now that I think about it, he must have been just as sure as Deer Pawn that you were still alive.

"He instructed us to follow the valley south. He also wanted us to scout around to see how much wildlife was in this part of the valley. With all the extra clan members plus all the new little ones we are having to spend more time looking for food. So, here we are my friend, now tell me about your journeys."

Just as Swims Like A Fish finished talking, Sabe and Oshkosh came out of the woods nearby. The new clan members raised their weapons and made ready to attack. But Talks With The Animals shouted to them to hold up. They stopped but none of them would lower their weapons. Swims Like A Fish had to tell them the story of how Sabe became a member of the tribe, but even after hearing the story the new clan members were uneasy. To them Sabe represented a large fierce animal that was very dangerous when confronted. Though they had not seen a Longnosed One in many years they still feared them.

Talks With The Animals spoke up. "I saw a small group of The Bearded Ones over by the river earlier. Let's go see if they are still there." With this everyone took off at a trot to find the herd. This was a hunting party and they needed all of the meat they could get. There were many little ones who needed food to survive.

They soon spotted the small herd, but could see no way to sneak up close enough to the animals to be in range to use their spears. The herd was out in the middle of a large opening and would take off as soon as the hunters showed themselves. Talks With The Animals had an idea. " I know what we can do," he said. He told the warriors to spread out on the downwind side of the clearing and wait. He would take Sabe and Oshkosh and circle around to the upwind side.

The smell of human, Longnosed One, and Singing Dog would surely set the herd to drifting downwind. When the time was right he and Sabe and Oshkosh would show themselves and drive the herd right into the waiting warriors. All they would have to do is stand up and attack the nearest animal to them. Everyone agreed that it sounded like a good plan.

The warriors placed themselves and Talks With The Animals took off to get upwind of the herd. When he was in position he stepped into the clearing with Sabe on one side and Oshkosh on the other. Both animals knew what was expected of them. The herd had already started moving downwind because of their smell. When they stepped out of the clearing the entire herd stopped eating and took off at a slow trot. Talks With The Wind gave a battle cry and took off after the herd.

Immediately afterwards Sabe trumpeted and Oshkosh howled and the both took off after Talks With The Animals.

The sight and sounds of the three caused the herd of Bearded Ones to panic and stampede right into the path of the waiting warriors. The warriors waited until the last minute to attack and took the herd by surprise. They managed to bring down several animals in the resulting melee. However, one of the warriors was caught in the side by the horns of one of The Bearded Ones. It tore a gash in his side several inches long, but luckily it did not penetrate very deep.

They set to work at once cleaning the animals and cutting up the meat. They had much more than they could carry, but Talks With The Animals told them not to worry. Sabe could carry a very large load. It took them several days to dry the meat but finally they were ready to return to the clan.

The wounded warrior was the only one without a pouch. He had recovered quite well from the nasty gash in his side, but he was not well enough to travel with a pouch yet.

Talks With The Animals was in a powerful big hurry to get home now that he knew Deer Pawn would be waiting for him.

He kept forging ahead of the hunting party and then stopping to wait impatiently for them to catch up. Swims Like a Fish could see that Talks With The Animals was in a rush to get back. He came up with the suggestion that Talks With The Animals take Sabe and Oshkosh and go ahead to the clan. They would be waiting for the meat. Since Sabe carried a large portion of it, it made sense for them to go ahead. The rest of the party would keep up a slower pace so the injured warrior would not fall behind.

Talks With The Animals agreed with this and took off at once for the clan. He traveled all night in his eagerness and came to the clan's camp soon after dawn the next morning. He went straight to his parent's camp and found The Wise One was already up and stirring around. His mother was also up and was busy cooking for the day. The Wise One looked his son over for a moment and approved of what he saw. His son had grown into a great warrior that he could be proud of.

He greeted Talks With The Animals as if he had just saw him yesterday. "Come and sit, we will talk while mother finishes preparing a meal." But When Talks With The Animals mother heard this she dropped everything and spun around quickly. Upon seeing Talks With The Animals she hurried over to hug him. The meal she was cooking was forgotten about in all of her excitement. Soon the odor of burning meat could be smelled. Deer Eyes suddenly realized the food was burning and hurried off to see after it. Presently she called out, "the food will be ready soon."

But Talks With The Animals was not thinking about food, he was thinking about Deer Pawn. He had not eaten since yesterday but that did not worry him. He had gone days without food before and would likely do so again. Finally, he could stand it no more. He stood up and told The Wise One that he must go and see Square Jaw right away. With this he was gone.

Chapter 11: Talks With The Animals takes Deer Pawn for his mate

Talks With The Animals quickly arrived at Square Jaw's camp. He saw Deer Pawn at once and suddenly stopped in his tracks. She was the most beautiful person he had ever seen.

She was tall and slender, and her clothes did not hide her full figure. Her skin looked silky smooth and had a deep tan from being in the sun. Her beautiful eyes looked him up and down quickly as if she were sizing up a rival. His heart was pounding as if he had been running as fast as he could go for a long time. Yet he was standing still. He wondered if Deer Pawn would really be happy to see him.

At first she just dropped what she was doing and stared. Then she cried out and made a mad rush after him. She did not stop until she was in his arms. She held on to him tightly and began to cry. "Oh, Talks With The Animals, I was afraid I would never see you again! I love you, Talks With The Animals, I have always loved you and I will always love you," she panted.

Talks With The Animals just held on tight. He was so choked up he could not speak. Finally he managed to squeak out, "I love you, too, and I will never leave you again as long as I live."

Deer Pawn's mother and father came rushing out to see what had startled her into crying out. "Well, don't just stand there gawking, Square Jaw." his wife said. "We have a lot of preparations to do, we must begin at once."

"What are you talking about woman?" Square Jaw asked.

"Can't you see, our daughter has found her man. We must begin making preparations for the ceremony. They will take a lodge together very soon."

After several minutes Deer Pawn and Talks With The animals broke apart and returned to where Deer Pawn's parents were standing. Square Jaw slapped Talks With The Animals on the back and said, "Come, we must talk to The Wise One. The women have much work to do. They set off to find The Wise One while the women got together and began talking excitedly.

Talks With The Animals awoke suddenly when he felt something hit him in the chest. He shook himself awake and grabbed at the arm he saw. Just as he was about to jerk the arm to throw his attacker off balance and give himself time to react he recognized the arm as Deer Pawns. Then it all came back to him. He now shared a lodge with Deer Pawn. This had been their first night together in their new lodge.

The last two weeks had been a blur. There had been much Celebrating, and there had been much to celebrate. First he had came home with many many pounds of meat. Only to be followed the next day with the arrival of the rest of the hunting party with even more meat. Two days later, there was the birth of another little one in the clan. The clan was now bigger than anyone could ever remember.

To top this off there was the celebration that always accompanied a man and woman taking a lodge together.

Talks With The Animals was very happy. He had the most beautiful woman in the clan for his woman. And not only was she beautiful, she was strong and healthy and he was sure she would bear him many healthy children. Deer Pawn awoke and looked into his eyes for a moment. She did not have to say anything, he knew how she felt because he felt the same way. She snuggled up to him and closed her eyes again.

Talks With The Animals just held her tight and thanked the Great Spirits for bringing her to him. After a while Deer Pawn awoke again and rolled over on top of him. He knew what she wanted and he was more than willing to oblige her. They spent the next day and night without ever leaving the lodge.

The next day a warrior came to their lodge and told Talks With The Animals that there would be a tribal council that night. The Wise One had something he wanted to say to the entire village. Talks With The Animals wondered what it was all about.

Finally everyone had arrived and formed a huge circle around The Wise One. He slowly rose to his feet and addressed the clan. "I have been thinking a lot lately," he said. "Our clan has prospered since coming to this great valley. There have been many little ones born in the few years that we have lived in the valley. In addition to this we have been joined by our brothers that came over the Great Hills just as we did. Because of this our clan has grown to the largest size that anyone can remember.

"Because there are so many people now, we must change our ways. This valley has given us our livelihood. It has provided us with food. It has provided us with clothing, and it provided protection from the weather. It has been a good home, and I want it to stay that way. Therefore we must change the way we do things.

"In the past we have always took what we wanted, when we wanted it. In the past we have killed animals strictly for sport, and not just for food. We will no longer do this. From this day forward we will only take what we need and nothing more. We will give thanks for what we have and we will give back to the valley each time we take something from it."

At this there was a lot of murmuring in the clan. Then The Lazy One stood and angrily stated that he would hunt and kill anything he wanted at anytime he wanted. He was his own boss and he would do whatever he wanted, The Wise One could not tell him what to do. There were several heads nodding in agreement with this. But the majority of the crowd just set quietly to see what The Wise One's response would be.

"The Wise One turned to face The Lazy One and calmly replied. "You are right, Lazy One, I cannot tell everyone in the clan how to live. I can only suggest and lead by example.

But I can tell you that we have always had to move from camp to camp in the past. Every time we move we would find a place that was teaming with animals. But every year we would have to travel further and further from camp in order to find meat for the clan. Until finally one day we have to travel so far that the whole clan would have to pack up all their belongings and move to another camp.

"What I am suggesting is that it is our own fault that we have to keep moving every few years to find food. Maybe we are killing the animals faster than they can have little ones of their own to raise.

The Lazy One spoke up again. "How do you know that? I do not think this is so. I saw a whole herd of The Longnosed Ones just the other day. And our hunting parties are almost always successful on the hunt. There is more food in this valley than we could ever use."

"Yes, it is true that our hunting is usually successful," The Wise One replied. "But it seems that each time a party goes on the hunt they have to spend more and more time traveling before they can find the herds again. All I am saying is that we should not waste anything. We should not kill if we do not need meat."

At this Square Jaw stood up and said, "The Wise One is right as usual. For who among us does not love the hunt? Who among us does not get a thrill at facing up to huge and dangerous animals like The Longnosed ones? Whose chest among us does not swell with pride when we have made a great kill? I for one love the hunt, but I can still see the wisdom of The Wise One. I had never thought of this before tonight, but now that I think back over the years I can see That The Wise One is right.

"I am considered a great warrior because I have led many hunting parties to a successful hunt. And I have personally killed many dangerous animals. I must admit that I like the thrill of the hunt. When we kill a dangerous animal everyone always comes and touches it to show that they are brave. Well, there is a way we can still hunt for sport and still not kill the animals."

At this, The Lazy One snickered. "What kind of person wants to hunt without killing? Where is the bravery in that?"

"I tell you where the bravery is in that," Square Jaw replied. Suppose we hunt down a herd of Longnosed Ones and instead of killing one of them and then everyone touching it, just suppose we go up and touch it without harming it in any way? Surely it would take a brave man to touch a Longnosed One while it is still alive and well. That would be much more dangerous than just touching one after it has already been killed."

There was a lot of discussion after this. The gathering lasted until dawn the next morning. It finally broke up with most of the warriors in agreement with The Wise One.

It was decided that the younger warriors that still needed to prove themselves could still hunt animals without killing them and still gain valuable knowledge and experience.

The next day Talks With The Animals ate a new food for the first time. It was yellow and had large seeds in it. He had never seen anything like it before. But it smelled good when it was cooking and most of the people in the clan loved it. The new clan members that had came over the Great Hills while he was gone had brought it with them. Or rather they had brought some seeds with them. They had learned to put the seeds in the ground at the beginning of the warm season. After a few moons the seeds grew in to a plant with great big leaves and then they would have flowers. After the flowers died the yellow fruit would grow.

Talks With The Animals had been skeptical when he heard this, but now he had seen it happen with his own eyes. Now here he was eating it so it had to be true. His wife had tended to plants. She gathered the berries and he hunted meat. That is the way it should be, he thought. His wife had much more patience with such things like picking berries. If he picked berries he would eat them all at once and there would not be any left most of the time.

Talks With The Animals was content. He was very happy with his mate. She was a very good cook. He leaned back to take a nap after finishing his meal. But Deer Pawn had other plans. She took his hand and led him to their lodge. They laid down next to each other.

Afterwards, as they were lying next to each other, Deer Pawn told him she had some news for him. Talks With The Animals told her to wait until later, he wanted to take a nap. However Deer Pawn insisted that she tell him now. Finally he gave in and told her to go ahead and tell him. She looked at him for a few seconds before answering him. "I am with child," she simply stated.

Suddenly Talks With The Animals was wide awake. "What did you say?" he asked.

"I said I am with child." she said again. Talks With The Animals grabbed her in a big bear hug and told her that he loved her. Just as quickly as he had grabbed her he let her go. "I am sorry, I didn't hurt you did I?"

"No," she replied. "I am not going to break into pieces just because I am with child.

Talks With The Animals jumped up and said, "we must spread the news. This is great, I am going to be a father."

Then he was gone to spread the news. Presently he came back home. But he was still excited. He suddenly wanted to do everything for her. But all he managed to do was to get in her way. Finally she had to send him away. "Go gather me some firewood, we will run out soon," she said. Talks With The Animals hugged her and was gone. He was so excited that he had to do something to work off his excitement. He made many trips back and forth gathering firewood. He was so excited that he worked all day without stopping. By the end of the day he had a pile of firewood bigger than their lodge.

He was going so strong that other members of the clan stopped what they were doing to watch him.

By the end of the day everybody in the clan knew that he was going to be a father. They had never seen anyone get worked up so much just on the news that they were going to be a father. To be sure it was a thing to be celebrated but there had to be an end somewhere. When night fell, Talks With The Animals was still too excited to sit still. He continued to gather firewood all night.

By the next morning there was so much firewood it totally surrounded their lodge. When Deer Pawn emerged from the lodge she did not have room to move. She called out to Talks With The Animals to stop bringing firewood and to make a path so she could move. Talks With The Animals had to move a large part of the brush he had collected again to make room around the lodge.

By the time he had cleared an area around the lodge, his night's work caught up with him. He lay down and closed his eyes at once. He did not awake until the next morning.

As time passed the excitement wore off and Talks With The Animals and Deer Pawn settled into a routine. Time passed quickly. They spent the whole winter making tools and clothing. Finally in early spring the little one arrived.

Once again Talks With The Animals ran around the village proudly announcing that he was the proud father of a baby girl. Deer Pawn had worried that Talks With The Animals would be disappointed because the child was a girl instead of a boy. But Talks With The Animals was thrilled, she had nothing to worry about. Besides she was still young and strong. There was still plenty of time to have another child. And though she did not know it she would in fact bear two strong sons in the future.

A few weeks after the little one was born, Talks With The Animals left with the other warriors to go on the hunt. They had almost run out of meat during the last cold season. Now fresh meat was needed more than ever. Along with Deer Pawn's child there were four more babies born that spring.

Talks With The Animals was disappointed. He was hoping to make a quick kill and return to his beloved wife. This was the first night they had not been together since they had taken a lodge together. He surely missed having her softness next to him. They were sure to make a kill tomorrow and he could return to his wife. But the hunting party did not make a major kill until three days later.

They finally located the herd of Longnosed Ones that The Lazy One had seen many moons before. There were seven or eight animals in the herd all together. It was hard to tell for sure. The animals tended to blend in with their surroundings from this distance. The hunting party was going to have to get much closer than this if they were going to capture any of these animals.

Square Jaw called all the warriors together for a small conference. They had to make a decision on how to best approach the herd. One of the warriors recalled that there was a small cliff only a few hundred yards from where the herd was feeding. If they were lucky they might be able to drive a couple of The Long Nosed Ones over the cliff. Talks With The Animals had brought Sabe and Oshkosh on the hunt as always.

They decided not to use Sabe on this hunt. They would be chasing after his own kin and Talks With The Animals was afraid that it might upset Sabe. Not only that, but the sight of

Sabe might make The Longnosed Ones turn and charge the warriors instead of running away. Sabe would have to stay behind on this one.

It was finally decided that each warrior would take a handful of straw and move into position. Most of the warriors would get in a position on the opposite side of the animals from the cliff, while a few more would line themselves up in a row on either side of the herd to drive them toward the cliff. When everyone was in position the signal would be given for the warriors behind the herd to set their straw on fire and charge the herd.

It was hoped that they could panic the herd enough to make it stampede headlong off the cliff. The plan had worked before so it should work here also. As long as the warriors on each side showed themselves at the right time they should be able to guide at least part of the herd off the cliff.

After making the plans, Square Jaw reminded everyone to be careful.

If one of the bulls broke away from the herd it was Okay. They did not need the whole herd anyway. In fact they really only needed a couple of animals. Once they had two over the cliff they would withdraw and let the remaining animals go. The meat from two animals would be all they could carry anyway. So there was no use in killing anymore than they had to.

Finally everyone was in place and the signal was given. The hunt was on. All the warriors lighted their grass and on the signal from Square Jaw they jumped into the clearing as one and began giving war whoops and waving the burning grass.

The herd of Long Nosed Ones stopped feeding at once and started moving away. Then the leader of the herd scented fire and panicked. She bellowed a warning and took off as fast as she could go. The entire herd took off after her.

Within seconds they were going full speed ahead. The larger animals began to pull away from the smaller ones and the herd ended up running in single file. Just as the leader of the herd started to veer off to her left. Another warrior stood up and began whooping and waving burning grass. This startled the herd and they just sped up even more. But their plan was working. They were able to guide the herd directly to the cliff.

When the leader saw the cliff she tried to stop, but it was too late. She plunged headlong over the cliff. The animals behind her were so frightened that they were not paying much attention to what was in front of them. Instead they were watching the dreaded fire behind them and running blindly ahead.

When the next animal saw the cliff the same thing happened. It tried to stop but it was just too late. When Square Jaw saw the second animal plunge over the cliff he immediately called off the hunt. They could not tote anymore meat than they would get from these two so there was no need to kill anymore. He understood this now, and so did most of the other warriors.

There was only one problem. Even though the warriors on either side of him stopped, the other warriors that had been placed on either side of the trail kept up the chase. Square Jaw noticed that they were the ones that had agreed with The Lazy One before. And since they were much closer to the cliff he did not have time to stop them. Square Jaw stood and watched helplessly as The Lazy One and his friends drove the entire herd over the cliff. He could see now that The Lazy One had tricked him.

When the warriors were assigned their positions for the hunt The Lazy One had volunteered himself and his brothers along with the few warriors that agreed with him to be stationed closest to the cliff. Square Jaw had assumed that The Lazy One did this so he could spend most of the hunt waiting, while the rest of the warriors chased the herd to the cliff. Then at the last minute The Lazy One and his friends would jump up and chase the herd the last few feet over the cliff and take credit for the kill.

That was typical of the way The Lazy One worked. But now he could see that The Lazy One had more than laziness in mind when he chose the position next to the cliff. He wanted to be sure that the entire herd went over the cliff. Square Jaw threw down his spear and took off after The Lazy One.

The other warriors followed close behind. The act of throwing his weapons on the ground was a direct challenge to fight.

Everyone in the tribe knew this and everyone also knew that The Lazy One was the one being challenged. As Square Jaw drew up in front of The Lazy One he swung a right fist directly into The Lazy One's face. The Lazy One went sprawling backwards and landed on his behind. Then he slowly fell over to the side. He was not seriously hurt but he would be out for a while.

Square Jaw looked at the other warriors and asked if anyone else wanted to question his command. No one took him up on the challenge. Square Jaw spoke menacingly, "I am in charge of the hunt and what I say goes. From here on anyone who does not follow my command will be left behind on the next hunt. Does anyone want to dispute this?" No one would argue with Square Jaw, especially after they saw how easily he had overpowered The Lazy One, who was a good warrior in spite of his laziness.

Then let's get to work, we have a lot of meat to prepare. We will only take meat from two of the animals. The rest of the herd will not be touched. At this there was some grumbling among The Lazy One's friends. "Anyone who does like the rules can step forward and discuss it with me," Square Jaw said. The warriors quickly stopped grumbling and made their way down to the bottom of the cliff. They set to work preparing the meat and hides at once.

On top of the cliff The Lazy One finally came to. When he realized that he was alone he got up to see where everybody was. He cautiously looked over the cliff and saw the warriors working on two of the animals. He started working his way down to the bottom of the cliff. Upon reaching the bottom he called to his friends. "Let the other warriors prepare the meat, we will go around and cut off the tusks to make weapons with.

His friends stopped working, but did not move when they saw that Square Jaw was approaching. Square Jaw ordered The Lazy One to get busy at once, but to work only on the two animals that were already being butchered. The Lazy One responded that he would take the tusks from the extra animals since it had been his work that resulted in the extra animals being killed. Once again Square Jaw swung his right fist and once again The Lazy One ended up on the ground out cold. Upon seeing this the other warriors went back to work.

Square Jaw spoke up again. "We will barely be able to carry the meat of two of The Long Nosed Ones back to the clan.

Can't you see that what you did wasted the meat of all the other animals? Their meat will spoil long before we could ever use it. Killing the other Longnosed Ones was a waste of time and meat. This will not happen again as long as I am in charge of the hunt."

The warriors worked over the meat for several days to get it prepared. The days were still very warm and during the hottest part of the day the smell from all the dead Longnosed Ones became overpowering. The Lazy One and his friends finally conceded that Square Jaw was right. They had been working furiously to get the meat prepared from the two animals they had butchered. Yet some of it still spoiled before they could get it all smoked. There was no way they could have prepared all of the meat from the other animals even if they had needed it.

Finally Square Jaw declared that they were ready to return to the clan. Everyone was relieved. No one enjoyed cleaning hides and smoking meat. This was work that the women usually did anyway. But they had to go so far from camp this time that the women stayed behind.

They packed up the meat and headed back to the clan. Had they known what lay in store for them that winter they might have tried to smoke meat from the other animals also. But they had no way of knowing that the herd of Longnosed Ones that they had just killed were the last herd on earth. There were no more. Sabe was the last living Longnosed One. They would find this out the next winter when they could not find enough food.

The hunting party returned to the clan exhausted and hot. Even with Sabe carrying a large portion of the meat, their packs on the return trip had been almost to heavy to carry. They had enough meat to last several moons. Some of it would be eaten now, but the plan was to save most of it for the coming winter. The women and children had been picking berries and roots while the warriors were gone.

Now with everyone here they decided to have a feast. And feast they did. Everyone gorged themselves to the limit, then they danced into the night. This went on for several days.

Finally the feast was over and the clan settled down into a normal routine. Instead of one large hunting party, one or two warriors went out at a time looking for The White Tailed Ones or the Bearded Ones. No one had seen any of the Bearded Ones in several moons now. They were bringing back The White Tailed Ones and other smaller game on a regular basis now.

In addition to this they collected acorns and ground them into meal. Overall during the warm season the whole clan ate quite well. But when the cold season arrived The Wise One realized there was not enough meat to last through the whole winter. He decided to send out a large hunting party one more time before snow fell in the valley.

The hunting party left with high hopes of finding a herd of The Longnosed Ones or maybe a herd of The Bearded Ones. But it was not to be. The party ranged far and wide but found neither The Longnosed Ones nor The Bearded Ones.

They did manage to find and kill a few of The White Tailed Ones and some other small game. But this would only add a few days' worth of food to their stores. The hunting party returned to the clan with very little to show for their efforts.

The Wise One was really worried now. They did not have enough food to make it through the winter. Maybe with a little luck they would have a mild winter and they would be able to go out all through the winter and find a little food here and there. But if the snows came early and piled up too deep they were in trouble. There could be mass starvation just as it had always been in the past.

The clan's luck did not hold. The snows came earlier and piled up higher than they had seen since entering the valley.

By mid winter the smoked meat from the two Longnosed Ones was nearly gone. They had only enough to last maybe one more moon at the best and maybe not even that long. But there were still two to three moons of cold weather left.

Slowly the clan began starving once again. Then one day the clan found one of their oldest members did not wake up from his sleep. The combination of cold and lack of food had been to much for him. The old and the very young were usually the first to die. The Wise One decided that they would have to try to find food again even though the snow was up to his waist. But instead of sending out one large hunting party they would send out several small parties. This way they could cover more area.

Each party would kill any of The White Tailed Ones they saw along with other small game. If they encountered a herd of Longnosed Ones or Bearded Ones they should send one member back to the clan for reinforcements while the other two followed the herd and left a trail for the other warriors.

The warriors split up into groups of three and set off into the woods. One such party consisted of Square Jaw, Talks With The Animals and Swims Like A Fish. They set off in a southerly direction. For the first few days they did not see any wildlife except birds and other small game. Finally they managed to kill one White Tailed One. But that was all the luck they had. They were so weak from cold and lack of food that they had to eat almost half of The White Tailed One before they made it back to camp.

They were the last hunting party to return. All of the other hunting parties had even worse luck than they did. Only two of the other five parties brought back any meat at all.

They were greeted with bad news upon their return. Several more clan members had died during their absence. One of them was Swims Like A Fish's little one.

Upon hearing this Swims Like A Fish cried out and set off at a dead run for his lodge. He found his woman lying with their stiff little one in her arms. He went to her and held her tightly and they mourned together.

Talks With The Animals hurried to his own lodge to see how his woman and little one was doing. He found Sabe standing quietly just outside his lodge as if he was guarding it. Sabe trumpeted happily when he saw Talks With The Animals.

This was the longest time the two had been separated since they started sharing a home together. Talks With The Animals stopped and petted Sabe and spoke softly to him for only a minute then he hurried on into his lodge.

Deer Pawn was sitting there holding their little one. Talks With The Animals heart felt like it was going to stop.

He thought the little one might be dead and he rushed to

113

Deer Pawn's side. He gasped out, "The little one, is she still alive?" Deer Pawn nodded her head yes.

"I have no milk," she said tearfully. "The little one has not had milk since yesterday. What are we going to do?"

Deer Pawn began to cry silently and Talks With The Animals held her closely. They sat that way for a long time. Then Sabe tried to poke his head in the door and nearly knocked the lodge down.

Talks With The animals got up and went outside to see to Sabe. "What is the matter Sabe?" He asked. He reached up to scratch Sabe behind the ear. Sabe was so tall now that he could barely reach high enough to scratch him. But it was still something that Sabe never seemed to tire of. Oshkosh lay at Talks With The Animals feet, just watching his master. Oshkosh was probably the only one in the village that was not in danger of starving to death. Even Sabe appeared to have lost some weight.

Talks With The Animals stood there until he was chilled to the bone. He talked to Sabe and Oshkosh as if they could understand every word he said. He told them about how he was worried, not only for the little one's life but for the life of Deer Pawn also. He knew that Deer Pawn was a strong woman, but if the little one died, the combination of starvation and losing the little one might be to much for her to take.

He was afraid that she might give up. If she did, she would surely die before the warm season returned. Somehow he felt that Sabe understood what he was saying. He felt much better after getting it all off his chest. Presently a warrior came by and told him that The Wise One wanted him to come to his lodge at once. Talks With The Animals became alarmed. His father would not call for him at a time like this unless something was really wrong.

He went back into his lodge and quickly built the fire up and told Deer Pawn he needed to go and see The Wise One.

He would be back shortly. He hurried out into the cold and went to The Wise One's lodge. The first thing he saw was his mother laid out on her skins. His father was lying next to her holding her hand. His younger sister was lying close by. His father looked up and shook his head.

"Talks With The Animals, your mother wanted to see you one last time before she leaves us. Come, speak with her now." Talks With The Animals went and knelt beside his father. He took his mother's hand and spoke to her. She opened her eyes and smiled, but she was too weak to speak. She squeezed his hand lightly then closed her eyes. She was no longer of this world, she had gone to the land of the great spirits.

Talks With The Animals sat with his father all night. Finally he got up and told his father he had to go and check on his own family. The Wise One understood. He merely nodded his head at Talks With The Animals, then he turned back to his mate. For him life would never be the same again.

Talks With The Animals was scared. His mother had just died. If The Wise One could not save her life, how could he possibly hope to keep his own family alive? When he arrived at his lodge Sabe gave him a happy trumpet in greeting as always. But for the first time Talks With The Animals did not respond.

When Sabe saw Talks With The Animals disappear into the lodge he picked up a small branch, shoved it into the lodge and dropped it at Talks With The Animal's feet.

This was his way of telling Talks With The Animals that he needed food. Talks With The Animals saw Sabe drop the branch and knew at once that Sabe was hungry. Talks With The Animals started to turn and return to his mate's side then stopped. Just because he was starving there was no need in letting Sabe starve also. He decided he would go ahead and gather branches for Sabe. Maybe if he was lucky he would find some small animal that he could carry back to feed his family.

He told Deer Pawn that he was going out to look for food one more time. He did not have anything to lose. He could starve in his lodge doing nothing or he could go out and try to do something about it. Well he might be hungry but he was still alive. Therefore he must try to do something to save his family.

He grabbed up his weapons and set out to look for food for Sabe and his family. Sabe and Oshkosh silently fell in behind him. An hour later Talks With The Animals had a whole armful of branches for Sabe. As he loaded them on Sabe's back Sabe suddenly dashed away from him. Sabe grabbed up one of Talks With The Animals spears only to return and drop it at Talks With The Animals feet and then he trumpeted excitedly.

Talks With The Animals looked at Sabe and tried to figure out what was wrong. Again Sabe picked up the spear and dropped it at his feet. "What is wrong with you, Sabe? Why are you acting so strangely?" Then Talks With The Animals suddenly remembered the time long ago when Sabe had charged full speed at him and spoiled his hunt long ago. At first he had been mad and lashed out at Sabe. It was only later that he saw footprints of the great cat which had been stalking him.

Talks With The Animals quickly picked up his weapons and started looking around for danger. But he could not see, hear or smell anything. And Oshkosh was lying around like everything was fine. Surely if there was danger in the area, Oshkosh would give him some warning. If anything Oshkosh's senses were even more keen than Sabe's were. Yet he sat by like nothing was wrong.

But Sabe was obviously excited by something. He spoke out loud to Sabe. "What is it Sabe? What do you sense that I or Oshkosh cannot smell?" At this Sabe trumpeted and turned away at a fast walk. After fifteen or twenty yards Sabe Stopped and looked at Talks With The Animals again. He trumpeted then started walking again. Talks With The Animals figured out that Sabe wanted him to follow him.

He took off after Sabe. But he was puzzled by Sabe's actions. Had Sabe seen a herd of animals somewhere and was trying to lead him to them? The only way to find out was to follow and see. Finally Sabe stopped near a cliff and trumpeted loudly. Talks With the Animals wondered what was up now. Surely Sabe knew he had to be silent or he would scare away any animals that might be close by.

Sabe looked over the cliff and trumpeted loudly again as if he was saying hurry up or you will miss it. When Talks With The Animals caught up to Sabe he looked over the cliff.

But all he could see below was a few boulders sticking up out of the snow. He looked at Sabe and asked him out loud again, "What are you trying to tell me, Sabe? There is nothing there to see." Sabe impatiently snatched a spear out of Talks With The Animals hands and dropped it at his feet again.

Talks With The Animals still did not understand. Always before when Sabe dropped something at his feet he either would drop a branch indicating that he was hungry or he would drop a weapon at his feet. Talks With The Animals had long since taught Sabe to fetch his weapons for him.

So Sabe obviously wanted him to use his spear for something, but what? There was nothing here to use it on. "Sabe, what has gotten into you?" he asked. He was wondering if maybe the cold and lack of food were affecting Sabe. But he had never seen Sabe act like this before. Sabe could take the cold better than he could. And even though Sabe had lost some weight this winter he had faired much better than he himself had. Suddenly Sabe picked up the spear once again and dropped it at his feet. Then he picked up a branch and dropped it at his feet to indicate food.

Talks With The Animals thought that was a sure sign that Sabe wanted him to use the spear to get food for something. Then Sabe lay down on his side with his belly facing Talks With The Animals. Suddenly it dawned on Talks With The Animals what Sabe meant. Sabe wanted Talks With The Animals to use the spear on him. But hungry though Talks With The Animals was he would never be able to do such a thing.

Suddenly Sabe got to his feet and trumpeted loudly. Then he turned and jumped off the cliff. Talks With The Animals realized too late what Sabe was up to. He screamed for Sabe to stop, but it was too late. Sabe was already falling over the cliff. Talks With The Animals heard a great thud and felt the earth shake. "No Sabe, no!" He called out. He looked over the cliff and could see Sabe lying at an awkward angle.

He was sure that Sabe's back was broken. He looked for a way down the face of the cliff, but it was too steep here.

The drop was only twenty feet or so but it was straight down. He would have to run back down the hill and circle around the base to get to Sabe. Talks With The Animals took off as fast as his legs would go in the deep snow. It took him fifteen minutes

117

to get to Sabe. But he was too late, Sabe was no longer of this earth. He shouted Sabe's name in rage and in sorrow over and over again.

He knew now for sure what Sabe had done. He had given his life so that his master and the others would live. With the end of Sabe's life The Longnosed Ones were no longer of this earth. Sabe had been the last Longnosed One alive. It was because of him and his people that Sabe was gone. Talks With The Animals vowed then and there that he and his people would never kill unless there was a need for food and clothing. They would never take more than they needed and they would strive to give something back. From now own they would do more than just live off the land. They would live with the land. They would do everything in their power to protect the land and all the life on it.

Talks With The Animals stayed with his friend and companion all night. He relived many of the good times they had together. Life would not be the same without him.

Finally the next morning he cut a large chunk of meat off and started back to the clan. With tears streaming down his face he struggled back to his lodge. He must not let the meat be wasted. Sabe wanted the clan to have the meat and he was not going to let him down.

He entered into his lodge and went at once to his mate's side. She was still sitting and holding the little one. Deer Pawn stared off into space as if she had given up hope. Talks With The Animals had to shake her gently to bring her out of it. Talks With The Animals looked into her eyes and smiled.

"We have meat, we are going to make it," he said. He turned and began cutting small strips of meat.

Deer Pawn had let the fire burn down to a bed of coals in Talks With The Animals absence. Talks With The Animals threw the strips of meat directly on the coals and they started sizzling almost immediately. The smell of cooking meat aroused Deer Pawn. Suddenly she was very alert. Talks With The Animals told her the meat would be ready shortly.

A few minutes later he began pulling out the smaller pieces and giving them to Deer Pawn. They were burnt on the outside and still nearly raw on the inside but Deer Pawn did not care.

Here was food. She must eat at once so she would have milk for the little one. The little one had drank water only for the last few days. It was very weak and would die soon without milk. Deer Pawn ate piece after piece of meat and drank great quantities of water. Finally Talks With The Animals would not let her have anymore for fear it would make her sick.

Deer Pawn lay down to build up her strength. She asked, where he got the meat from.

All Talks With The Animals would say is that Sabe led him to it. It was all he could to do keep from crying out again. Talks With The Animals had never known pain like this before. He had been wounded many times but that was nothing like the ache he felt in his chest for Sabe. He said, "You can thank Sabe when you get stronger." He had already decided not to tell Deer Pawn just where the meat came from.

He knew that she had become quite attached to Sabe and Oshkosh and might not eat the meat if she knew the truth.

He knew he would never be able to eat the meat. He would rather die. He knew Sabe wanted him to eat the meat but he just could not do it. "I must go tell the rest of the clan about the meat. I will be back before the day is over.

Talks With The Animals went and gathered up Square Jaw, Swims Like A Fish and a few other warriors he knew could be trusted. He told them to come with him. He had found enough meat to last the rest of the cold season. After leaving the clan he stopped the party and told them what had happened. He knew most of the warriors would recognize Sabe so he might as well tell them ahead of time so they would be prepared. It was agreed that they would not tell the rest of the clan where the meat came from. Sabe had become an accepted member of the clan. There was no use upsetting the people any more than necessary. They would only tell that Sabe had led them to the meat.

It took the warriors two days to get the meat back and distributed to the whole clan. For one more member of the clan the food came too late. But the rest of the clan made it through the winter thanks to Sabe. Finally, one day the snow began to melt and the grass started to grow again.

Talks With The Animals was struggling to keep up a happy

face around Deer Pawn. She and the little one were doing fine. For this he would be forever in Sabe's debt. But he sure missed Sabe. Even Deer Pawn had asked about him several times. Finally he told her that Sabe had gone to bewith his own kind. They would never see him again. "So that's why you have been so sad lately," she said. "I thought maybe I had done something wrong."

Talks With The Animals took Deer Pawn in his arms held her close for a long time. "No, my beloved. I am very happy with you," he said softly.

Chapter 12: The Clan splits up

One day early in the warm season The Wise One called for the entire clan to gather for tribal council. Talks With The Animals was worried. His father did not seem to be too well.

It appeared that the winter had been too hard on him. However it was not the harsh winter but the passing of his mate to the great spirits that was wearing The Wise One down.

Once again the entire clan gathered around to hear what The Wise One had to say. The Wise One stood slowly and addressed the clan. "Brothers, I am getting old. I am no longer able to fulfill my duties as The Wise One. It is time to pass my duties on to someone more able to handle the task.

This is not an easy job but among us we have people capable of doing the job." He stood looking at the Great Hills that surrounded the valley for a few minutes.

Finally he continued his speech. "But before I turn this position over to someone else I must tell you all a story. It was told to me by The Wise One before me; and it was told to him by The Wise One Before him. It has been so for many generations now. Now I must tell the story to the whole clan. It is an important story and it is a true story. I charge each and every one of you to listen to this story and to learn from it."

And so The Wise One told the story of his grandfather's grandfather. He told the clan about the far away land that existed on the other side of the great water. He told them how there came to be too many people and how they were on the brink of starvation because there was not enough food to go around. He told them about how the people had split up and how some of them traveled across the land that rose up out of the sea.

"We are the descendants of those people that came across the land that rose out of the sea. It seems that we have not learned a lesson from this. But I think there is a great lesson to be learned from this and I will tell you what it is.

For as long as I can remember our clan has had to move

121

every few years. Most of you are old enough to remember the long walk over the great hills that brought us to this valley.

Some of you can remember the long walk that took us to the great cave where we lived for years before we came here.

"It has occurred to me that each time we move to another location we find plenty of wildlife to eat. But with each passing year there seems to be less and less wildlife around where we live. It was true when we lived at the great cave and it is true here is this valley. Who among us can not remember the great abundance of wildlife that was here in the valley when we arrived?

Where has it all gone? I will tell you where it has gone. We have destroyed it. Yes people, you and I have destroyed it. We have traditionally taken what we wanted, when we wanted. And we have not given anything in return.

We must change our ways. We must learn to give something back to the land. We must learn that there must be places that are for wildlife only. We must learn not to abuse the land. In short, we must take care of the land if we want it to take care of us. I can assure you that one will not happen without the other.

"As most of you know we just barely made it through the last cold season. There was not enough food to go around. If it had not been for Talks With The Animals finding meat most of us would have starved before the warm season returned. As it is one fourth of us went to the great spirits in the sky during the cold season.

"So, once again we have gone full circle. Once again we find ourselves needing to move again. But where will we go?

How many more places like this valley are out there? This I do not know. But surely if we keep on the way we have in the past we will one day run out of great valleys like this one.

I tell you one and all, we must change our ways. From this day forth I charge each and every one you with the responsibility to take care of the land. We must not take more than we need. And we must give back to the land when we can. We must be keepers of the land.

"And now I would like for Square Jaw, Talks With The Animals, and Swims Like A Fish to join me." At this, the three who were summoned, got up and joined The Wise One in the center of the clan. "Swims Like A Fish, I know that you lost your child during the cold season. My little one survived, but I am no longer able to look out for her without my mate at my side. I charge you with raising him as if he were your own child."

Swims Like A Fish was stunned. "Yes Wise One." he managed to say. At this there was a great murmuring among the clan. The Wise One raised his hands for silence. I am old and feeble. It is my wish that Swims Like A Fish and his mate look after my little one. Swims Like A Fish, you may return to your seat.

And now, Square Jaw and Talks With The Animals, I have an important charge for both of you. Once again we must split the clan up just as our grandfather's grandfather did many generations ago. Talks With The Animals, you will lead the part of the clan that will leave the valley. Square Jaw you will be the leader of the clan members that stay behind. From this day forth you will both be known as The Wise One in your own clan."

Square Jaw started to protest but he was cut off by The Wise One. "I have spoken. It will be so." With this The Wise One left the crowd and returned to his lodge. The people of the clan milled around for a while and then finally returned to their lodges.

Talks With The Animals clasped his father's arm tightly. He knew he would never see him again. Slowly he turned to look over his people one last time. There was nothing else he could do. The people were ready to travel. They must leave now if they wanted to get to the little valley by the great river where he had spent the winter alone before the next cold season arrived.

He was already tired but he knew he would make it. He had been pushing his people to get ready to travel since the day after his father had given his speech. Almost a full moon had passed since then. It would take them several moons to reach their destination. He was confidant there was plenty of food there for his people. Not only would they be able to find food on the way. But once settled in they could plant the seed of the yellow food he had become so fond of.

He said one final farewell to his father, Square Jaw, and the rest of the clan that would remain in the great valley. Then he raised his arm to signal that he was ready to move out. He lowered his arm and started moving south.

This was going to be a long journey. Traveling this way alone was one thing, but doing so with women and the little ones would be another story. At least he knew where he was going this time. And he was fairly well stocked with food.

The berries were just turning ripe now so they would find food along the way.

Talks With The Animals led his band south through the valley. He had Swims Like A Fish at the back end of the clan to make sure no one was left behind. It sure was a relief to have someone like Swims Like A Fish helping. He was a good warrior and getting better every day.

After traveling for two days they encountered the natural stone bridge at the southern end of the valley. He stopped the clan here for the night. Then he went to climb the stone bridge. When he reached the top he sat down to look out over the great valley. He could spend hours up here looking and never get tired of the view.

He could see all the way up the valley. Up above he could see a couple of birds lazily circling on the rising wind. He could hear more birds chirping among the trees as they went about their lives. The great hills in the distance took on a hazy blue color during the heat of the day. He was going to miss this valley.

So far they were making good time. They were even traveling faster than when he came this way alone. But this time he knew exactly where he was going. He did not have to explore every side valley or stream he came to.

The next day the clan was up at dawn and moving out again. Finally they passed out of the great valley into the smaller valley. But Talks With The Animals did not let up. He kept the clan moving day after day.

They finally reached the stream that Talks With The Animals knew was the start of the great river. He decided to let the clan rest for a couple of days. Besides they needed to find meat before they ran out. They had been able to kill a couple of The White Tailed ones but that just was not enough.

He sent Swims Like A Fish out to hunt while he stayed behind to look after the clan. He would much rather be out hunting with Swims Like A Fish but his duties were here with the clan. After looking after Deer Pawn to make sure she was okay he made the rounds to the rest of the clan.

He stopped by The Lazy One's lodge to see how his family was doing. The Lazy One's family had been the hardest hit from the last cold season. His mate was one of the people that did not survive the winter. The Lazy One was a changed man after that. He was getting on in years yet he did every thing he possibly could to help his family. And he had not complained once. Talks With The Animals almost wished that the old Lazy One would return. He sure used to be good for a laugh every now and then. Of course he used to be a headache also. He decided the clan was better off with the new Lazy One.

The next day Swims Like A Fish returned with his hunting party. They had been successful. They managed to bring down two of The Bearded Ones. There would be enough meat to get the clan through to his little valley.

After a few days the clan was on the move again. It was very hot during the day now and it made the traveling that much tougher. And the insects could be down right mean sometimes. However the clan was in quite good spirits.

They were seeing signs of wildlife everywhere. Each day the stream grew bigger as the made their way down stream. One day Talks With The Animals called the clan together for a meeting.

He was The Wise One now and it took some getting used to. He stood and addressed the clan. "We have only a few more days to go and we will be there."

When he said this one of the younger warriors stood up and said, "What's wrong with where we are at now? I see wildlife all around us. Why not just stay right here?"

Before The Wise One could answer him The Lazy One spoke up. "Because he is the wise one and we will do like he says. Now sit down and be quiet before your mother tans your hide."

At this the clan began laughing and the young warrior sat back down. Some day he would be older and wiser like The Lazy One, but it would take many years.

Four days later around mid day, Talks With The Animals held up his hand to stop the clan. The warriors hurried up to see why he had stopped the clan in the middle of the day.

He declared, "We are here. All we have to do is climb this next ridge and we will see the little valley." The warriors started whooping and ran back to their families to give them the good news. The people were so excited they virtually ran all the way up the ridge. Finally they came to the top of the hill.

There before them on both sides of the great river stretched a beautiful little valley. They could hear birds singing, and see small animals scurrying about their business. Next to the river they could see a couple of The White Tailed Ones.

And across the river they could see a small herd of The Bearded Ones feeding peacefully on the lush grass. Talks With The Animals heard a splash in the water and looked just in time to see one of the big Striped Fish fall back into the water.

Talks With The Animals was home. He knew he would never leave this little valley. He vowed to protect it. He would give his life for it if necessary. For he new that the valley would give him a life as long as he took care of it. He must spend his life teaching his people to be keepers of the land.

Chapter 13: Bob leaves the cave.

Bob stood up. He had been sitting there listing to Charlie for a long time. Finally Charlie had fallen silent. Bob was sore from sitting still for so long. He walked to the front of the cave to relieve himself. He was startled to see daylight outside. He must have sat there all night listening to Charlie's story about his ancestors.

He walked back into the cave where Charlie was lying quietly. Charlie must be really tired to fall asleep that soon after talking to him. In fact Charlie was not making any noise at all. Bob went to his side and knelt down. He did not see Charlie breathing. He felt for a pulse. There was none. Bob's first thought was he is no longer of this world. He had gone to join the great spirits in the sky.

Suddenly Bob knew what he had to do. Somehow he knew the story he was just told was true. He must go back to his own people and tell this story. He must tell all the whites about the legend of the landkeepers. He must warn his own people that they too must learn to care for the land. Or one day there may not be enough food to go around.

Bob stayed in the small cave for two months before the weather cleared enough for him to leave. He placed Charlie's remains at the back of the cave. Old Charlie Landkeeper had finally gone to the spirit world to be with his beloved wife and child.

Bob would spend the rest of his life trying to educate the white man. Though he never became famous as a wildlife preservationist he would have a very important effect on the future of the world's wildlife.

In just a few years he would go on a journey with John James Audubon to tour the great western United States, and describe the wildlife found there.

About the Author

RUFUS JOHNSON was born in Northampton County , North Carolina, in 1958. He attended Halifax Community College in Weldon, North Carolina. He has had several articles published in different magazines. He currently lives in Roanoke Rapids, North Carolina.